Twilight of the Gods: Book of Skuld

Book 3 of Odin's Sacred Runes

Nathan Anderson

Edited by: D. Kupke

Book cover artwork: D.C. Wince

Copyright © 2023 Nathan Anderson

All rights reserved.

ISBN: **9798388812247**

DEDICATION

This book is dedicated to my beautiful daughters, Charli and Bonnie. Know that true beauty is a nature and not how we appear to others. May life grant you wisdom to see beyond the superficial nonsense others allow you to see.
May your hearts love with strength and your lives be filled with honour whatever path you decide to take. The future is yours, embrace it and make it your own. Our destination has already been written but our actions write our stories in the present. You can create your own legacy. It won't be easy but nothing worthwhile ever is. Hold onto Hope with Honour and share a few Ho Ho Hos on the way.

CONTENTS

	Acknowledgments	i
1	Introduction	Pg 3
2	Skuld is Known	Pg 6
3	Falling Like Snow	Pg 8
4	Christmas Kraken	Pg 11
5	No Time for Heroes	Pg 15
6	The Fall of the Gods	Pg 18
7	Under the Mistletoe	Pg 23
8	Regain your innocence	Pg 28
9	Yule's Magic is Lost	Pg 34
10	The Ghost of Christmas Past	Pg 39
11	Cailleach (Auld Lang Syne)	Pg 53
12	A Dark winter's Night	Pg 59
13	Sinterklaas	Pg 65
14	Yule Cats	Pg 70
15	Gríðr and the Yule Lads	Pg 73

16	Tomtenisse	Pg 77
17	Scrooge (Lokasenna)	Pg 81
18	The Wild Hunt	Pg 90
19	Dashing Through the Snow	Pg 95
20	Fimbulwinter	Pg 100
21	Silent Night	Pg 107
22	Ragnarök	Pg 111
23	Happy Yule (war is over)	Pg 116

ACKNOWLEDGMENTS

Padraic Colum and PogányW. (2019). *The children of Odin : the book of northern myths*. New York, N.Y.: Aladdin

Snorri Sturluson and Arthur Gilchrist Brodeur (2010). *The prose edda : tales from Norse mythology.*

Larrington, C. (2019). *Poetic Edda.* Oxford University Press.

Saxo, G. and Hansen, W.F. (1983). *Saxo Grammaticus & the life of Hamlet : a translation, history, and commentary.* Lincoln: University Of Nebraska Press.

Reaves, W.P. (2018). *Odin's Wife*. Amazon: KDP self-publishing, p.363

i

Introduction

In 2018 I found the Norse gods and their stories via YouTube short videos. From there I found the Eddic poems and then the mysteries behind skaldic poetry thanks to Snorri Sturluson. After understanding that a horse was not simply a horse according to the ancient kennings in poetry, I realised that even the ancient texts were open to interpretation.

Norse characters seemed to change their name frequently, depending on their story and the meaning behind it. Each name behind the character going by that name hinted at a linguistic representation of something much deeper. It appeared that the fantastic stories of Odin and his children along with other gods and goddesses had more than surface entertainment.

I struggled with the cryptic clues of what Runes and Seidr magic could possibly mean in terms of modern representation through an ancient description of the applications. Once I found out a possibility it made sense to link the Norse stories in chronological order while combing similar tales that appeared to be fragmented through the years of only verbally passing them on. Suttung and Thyazi, Gulveig and Angerboda, Gunnlod and Skadi, each of these characters seemed oddly similar in description.

Moving from Scandinavia to way beyond became easier with the diversity of the Jotun race. Mainly humanoid type monsters, but not limited to, would allow me to branch into other civilisations and their stories. Jormungandr had similarities in other parts of the world when it came to a serpent/ dragon/ sea creature tied to the oceans or storms. Tales of Yeti, bigfoot or even Yowie sightings suggest although the names may differ from region to region each culture had similar characters.

Connection to the extraordinary world we live in was another proud moment when completing this trilogy series. The word realms being a synonym for lands made me wonder if it wasn't cosmic or dimensional realms but simply the descriptions of types of land masses that exist in the world during ancient times.

Was Vanaheim like Atlantis due to the connection with Njord? Was Muspelheim like the Volcanic desert in the Sahara? Was Jotunheim rocky and mountainous terrain and was Svartalfheim like caves in dark forest-type lands? Was Alfheim the secret city of Eldorado due to the bright beautiful creatures that inhabit there? Niflheim was cold and icy like Antarctica. Was Helheim a hidden gateway to Niflhel the realm of the dead? Was Midgard everywhere in between these enchanted and sometimes dangerous places? Places humans fought hard to survive those other harsh and dangerous landscapes. And finally Asgard, any pantheon that has existed has always had a place above the lands in the skies. Olympus, heaven or Valhalla all seem to exist above like one must ascend to get there.

Landscapes were more segregated when the world was a supercontinent called Pangaea. Over time, the world has become more spread out with the landscapes mixing and diluting amongst the continents while they drifted to their present position. These tales diluted or evolved similarly to the landscapes of the world. Using this story helped me bring together places in the world like the Great Wall of China, the pyramids even the Grand Canyon.

Tales from my mythical homelands of Scotland and my new home of Australia are all connected despite the thousands of miles they are separated by on the map. It sparked the whole concept of how stories connect the world. Egyptian and Greek stories inspired me to show the evolution of tales throughout religion.

Diving into the darker side of Christianity, the testaments removed, the book of Enoch, the tales of archangels and Lucifer's attempt at claiming heaven. Even the fact that in Christianity it was God that created the leviathan and behemoth the Christian counterparts of Jormungandr and Fenrir. It made me wonder if Lucifer/ Loki found a deceitful way of taking the throne of Asgard away.

Moving away from religion I found other mythological links throughout traditions to the holidays that even Christianity has adapted to fit its own ideals. However, the traditions and practices we have today never actually matched up with biblical stories. Plot holes became larger in a story simply followed by many.

Christmas seemed to be adapted from Yule and the myths surrounding Yule had more to do with modern Scandinavian and Germanic roots than anything related to Christianity. The shepherds out with their flock suggest the time of year of Jesus' birth was more in the spring/ summertime. The three wise men described as Magi (magic users) were more mysterious than simple kings.

I used the character of Sinterklaas, Santa Claus and every other bearded mage-type character that appeared to guide heroes or educate them to their purpose as many of the titles Odin used to guide warriors on their path. The darker side of Santa Claus suggests he not only gifted gold as a dowry for a poor man's three daughters, he also resurrected three children from death. Necromancy would have been against Christian beliefs but for a god linked to death, war and wisdom it would have been easy. The three children took vengeance on their killer who appeared to be a horrible innkeeper. Even the fact that the church tried to dethrone Santa and replace him with Jesus under the name of Kris Kringle made me ask why?

The Germanic name of Thor and the representation of Mjolnir made me think there is more to Santa than meets the eye. The Nordic translation of Odin's horse (that may not be a horse) describes the function of a sleigh. Eight legs linked to Eight characters and their weapons or stories linked to modern myths fascinated me. Mistletoe linked to Baldur, Frau Holle, the wild hunt and even the Havamal has stanzas on gift giving. Did Odin evolve into Santa for a reason?

The world remains ignorant of the sources and possible links to the origin of Santa. Perhaps I felt the need to explain the power behind such an influential character that has survived the ages by inspiring children through the magic of imagination and gift-giving.

For three years I have managed to complete essentially the bones of the Edda fleshed out by using myths, religion and the realisation that the world is too complex for a simple right vs wrong. Delivering the Hávamál in a way that gives an entertaining tale while revealing the character of Odin was the icing on the cake for me. It outlined how to conduct oneself in a variety of situations while also revealing parts of the story.

A trilogy series that will hopefully bring the world together through its own diversity and through a connection to ancient tales. This was a journey of self-discovery that I am grateful for. Five years ago I never knew I could write and now I've released a trilogy book series and a nonfictional collection relating the gods to my life. I am humbled by my experience and enjoy delivering such a unique story.

Skuld is Known

Greetings good host. The world is a cold place now, can you feel it? People are scrambling over each other to survive. Lying has become most people's first language and even a picture masks the truth. The only thing a filter does is remove respect for yourself. The world is on the brink of collapse and people are too ignorant and foolish to realise it.

Life has become darker under Fimbultyr's or the great God's rule. The value of someone's word has become worthless. The phrase "I promise" isn't honoured as much as it should. Even love itself is used more frivolously, so that it too has lost its magickal value. The world as we know it has lost its wonder and that is why I have wandered back.

How does an old weary man become more, more than just an old man with a great tale? Well, it was with the god-life I had sacrificed I had gained the wisdom required. The wisdom of the Runes is not as superficial as a generic and cryptic affirmation tied to a letter meaning. It is magic known only to those that bleed onto the pages of history. Those that live epic stories that others write and embellish. Humans become something much more than their mortality can gift. Heroes become legends and legends can sometimes rise higher than even gods.

The Runes are marked on our bodies and souls, like a scar from the Norns. The past, the present and the future test us, challenge us, and force our growth through difficulties. There are three types of scars that the Norns write and we must endure them to become wise in this world. Physical scars provide stories of survival. Mental scars that provide awareness and adaptability. The emotional trauma that gifts us direction in life. The things we like and situations we don't, help us get back to our path when sometimes we stray. The Runes or letters help us write and record moments whether it be enhanced by fantasy or not, the magic between the words is the message you wish to leave.

With letters, you can conjure a word. With words, you can create a sentence. With sentences, you can cultivate paragraphs. With paragraphs, you can manifest chapters. And with chapters, you can enchant a story. That is the power writers and storytellers have, good host. I have created tales to inspire, and words to encourage those low of spirit. I have manipulated your mind and created lands in your imagination filled with creatures from all over the world. The wisdom of the Runes is letter by letter, word by word the building blocks of story writing.

Nothing is more complex than life, good host. It is more beautiful because of the contrast. We can't understand great joy if we haven't experienced great loss. We can't appreciate our lives if we remain ignorant of death. Take it from an old man that has created life and taken it away. The knowledge we gain through life is the in-between. Perceptual wisdom is yours alone but remains open to understanding and you become almost god-like.

Allow me to tell you about some of the thousand lives I have lived. The ones that I have shared over the many years I have existed. You will have heard of my tales as I have gone by many names, too many to count. I've existed in the shadows and right in front of your face. I have existed as many old men over the years and sometimes even inspiring women from time to time. Each of my lives has its unique tales but everything must end, good host, including me.

When facing the overwhelming might of a superior enemy you must use their overconfidence as their weakness. The greatest trick Loki ever made, was when he used Tacitus to convince the world he did not exist. The greatest lie he ever told was in his book, when he convinced the world he was all good.

Allow me to tell you of a time when I reclaimed Asgard. I will also explain the hard times that will come. Not all will survive, good host, but if I can leave you with anything, it will be the realisation of the importance of life and the will to live. Hold on to hope with honour, good host. And don't forget to share a few ho ho hos along the way.

Falling Like Snow

Many years have passed since I hung from the great tree, and many more had come to be when I lurked in the ocean as a sea monster. I had claimed so many lives unfortunate enough to seek refuge on an island that was not as it appeared. I may have seemed like an oasis in the vast ocean but what lay beneath would rob most heroes of their courage. My tentacles took hold of mighty ships and dragged them to the depths and filled Aegir's Hall.

While I floated on the surface, unable to return home, Loki made his attempt to claim Asgard. You may or may not have heard the tales of Lucifer, but this is what the Christians called him. Loki gathered what creatures he could muster to conjure an army. Any Jotuns or dark elves that could be convinced by the forked tongue of Loki would become part of his demon army. After he gifted them the power that made them more menacing, they made their way to Asgard's border to unleash their onslaught on the gods.

Loki became similar to the Trojan horse, in Greek myth, in this situation. He looked like me and sounded like me too. Asgard's defences would have been cautious with Loki, but to me, they lowered their guard. It was wise that the gods and Valkyrie remained vigilant in Loki's presence because you could never tell what kind of problems he would cause. Unfortunately, he was welcomed in Asgard and as the gods, Valkyrie and elves were distracted the demons gathered, ready to attack. Never be so foolish as to trust someone like Loki fully, because their past has not made them wiser, only more cunning.

Appearing as their king, Loki lured the gods into dropping their defences and awareness. Thor was also absent and was unable to protect them. Loki had the power to enter regardless but the goal wasn't to simply exist amongst the gods rather he wished to claim the control that comes with Hlidskjalf. All I was able to do in my monstrous form was watch, through my mind's eye. I observed his actions in the present and knew the past that lead him there.

The demons began their attack with ruthlessness and efficiency. Their numbers were vast and their size and magical powers proved challenging. However, the gods were still too powerful defending the Skylands. Each demon that attacked was slain and fell from Loki's power and grace. They plummeted back to Jotunheim or Svartalfheim and remained in the darkness. Some even joined my brother Surtr in Muspelheim.

Loki's army of monsters and demons provided a great test of the gods' resolve and their mighty weapons in the absence of knowledge. However, when they appeared to lose, Loki unleashed his greatest ally. It was a beast with power, even more, mightier than his. A dragon from the roots of Yggdrasil itself. One of his fathers tried to gain its allegiance before and it left him burned with charred flesh. It was Nidhoggr.

The dragon that started it all. From the time of Ymir and Audumla, slowly it has been gnawing the roots of the world tree. It never favoured the ignorant Vili so why would it aid Loki? Perhaps it was because Loki had the power of Verdandi and Urd. You can create any future you desire if you have the past, the present and time itself at your disposal. The wisdom from the past, the power of the present and time on your side are enough to defeat most but Frigg and I strategically prepared for the attack.

You might have heard the tale as Archangel Michael's but, in truth, that story was adapted from Baldur's. This was also Loki's great trick. He twisted the ancient tales of paganism to fit the twisted beliefs his church wished to conjure. Adam and Eve with Askr and Embla, the devil would come from the north and I enjoyed my stay at the North Pole. There were many tales and traditions tied to Loki's religion that have many pagan origins. Look a little deeper and the answers may reveal themselves.

Returning to the battle in Asgard, Baldur had faced a dragon long ago when he was known as the mortal Sigurd. This time he would face the beast as an invulnerable god. Flame met flesh protected by magic and sword and claws clashed. It was a glorious battle that would be told many times under many names as heroes or kings. Nidhoggr was much larger than Fafnir was and he struck with much more malice.

With every attack, Baldur smiled and shrugged it off as nothing. Having the power of the helm of awe imbued within, he was unable to take or feel the effects of any damage. Nidhoggr's teeth and claws became blunt with every strike the dragon took. The glorious Baldur fought valiantly, laughing in the face of the beast's assault.

As victory seemed to be in the favour of the gods, Loki enhanced the dragon's power further, in attempt to turn the outcome of the battle around. One head was replaced by three and Nidhoggr became Zmei Gorynich. The extra challenge didn't faze the shining god, he was essentially invulnerable. Flame consumed him but he walked through the fire unaffected by its blaze. With two swings of his sword, the beast was returned to its original headcount. Excalibur was pointed at Nidhoggr's head. The blade was honed to the point and sharper than Loki's powerful wit.

"You have no power here, dragon! Return to the hole you crawled from and I will spare your life."

"Asgard is lucky to have such a formidable warrior defending it. The victory is yours, son of Odin but you won't be around forever. And when you fall, I will return to burn everything you hold dear. When the world is scorched and the dead are draped from my wings, you will respect my power, little god."

"Return to your roots worm, while I allow it!" Baldur demanded with Excalibur at the ready.

Nidhoggr was no fool. He retreated and slithered down towards Midgard. The great dragon borrowed himself deep beneath the soil. My Frigg closed the earth behind the great beast, sealing him in his prison until Ragnarok begins. With blunted teeth, the dragon returned to gnawing the root of Yggdrasil. Slowly biding his time amongst the roots of the great tree until Ragnarök was upon us.

With the wisdom I shared with Forsetti long ago, he saw the truth behind Loki's disguise. Loki may have assumed my image but the gods understood that character was more important. Regardless of the former position, a leader must honour their duties in the present. For if they slip or prove themselves unworthy of leadership they don't deserve the responsibility to lead. Forsetti spoke clearly in his judgement and Loki was expelled from the Skylands, never to be welcomed back.

This would force Loki to apply more devious methods to remove the gods from their position. In the minds of the mortals, he would demonise and vilify my sons and make the world turn from my rule. A goat-headed creature linked to Satan's image would be his attempt to turn the people away from Thor and me. They would seek a weaker more peaceful "god" to rule the heavens above. An absent god blind to the world's delicate balance between life and death. A god that renamed blind luck into magic known as miracles.

The Christmas Kracken

Cursed to a monstrous form to float in the vast emptiness of the deep blue sea. With no land in sight and only the sea creatures as company, I was alone with my thoughts, unable to escape them. Sometimes they would consume and torture my happiness, but I welcomed the rest. I needed it to concoct my plan. A plan that may take millennia to execute effectively. After all, I made oaths when I ruled and if I never kept them I wouldn't be worthy of respect from anyone.

Sometimes there would have been a few unfortunate sailors that drifted my way and sought sanctuary from the perilous ocean. However, the nature of a Kraken isn't so friendly. My long serpent-like arms and legs wound and weaved beneath the surface. Delicately dancing to the depths until weary ships approached my back. I'd simply watch from the silent abyss beneath the waves. I could feel the vibrations in the water as the ripples on the surface came to rest on my back.

Each boat that drifted into range was tricked with the illusion of rest and salvation. However, when they got close enough to realise what the island was it was already too late. I splintered the ships and collapsed the masts. The sounds of crunching and cracking forced the mortals to take their chances with the unforgiving Ran and her razor-toothed children. I supplied many servants to Aegir and Ran's hall during those years.

Now and then my lady, my beloved would visit. Despite my hideous appearance and horrible nature, she still loved me. It broke my heart that I couldn't hold her like I used to. I couldn't feel the warmth of her touch or the softness of her lips. Curses appear to be a fate worse than death at times, but it is only through our troubles we grow mentally strong. To be a monster that could only protect our sacred place from unwanted attention from the outside world was not desired, but it is a time some must endure. She was my heart and as long as I lived, in this form, I would provide her with a safe place to be with me. It was the least I could do, she was my future and got me through the tough times.

Years went by and the volume of sailors became scarce as the stories began spreading throughout Midgard. The majority of my time was spent alone and during one such time, a boat approached. Such a little vessel but the crew is always what makes the voyage worthwhile. I had assembled the team myself from the shadows for this exact purpose. To slay the Kraken and release my soul from my monstrous form.

One sailor would plan the attack. Another would deliver a blow that would lift my head and eye above the surface and a hero to render my monstrous size harmless. Theseus was the king to plan and plot. Thor was the god to deliver the blow with his hammer. Perseus, with Medusa's head, would freeze my giant body and encase it in stone. A deceptive island would become nothing more than a solid rock. It would allow sailors to explore the oceans with one less threat at least.

The small boat moved steadily towards me. The temperature dropped slightly as the cool rain fell on my back. The skies darkened as the thunder rumbled in the distance. I was prepared to die that day, even if it was at the hand of my son. There is peace and rest in solitude but there comes a time that even that has to end. I had a job to do, a heart to warm and an oath to fulfil.

"We need to bring its head above the surface. I have an idea, but I have to ask, how much strength can you muster Heracles?" Theseus asked as they drifted closer to danger.

"We are far from Fjalar's inn, good king. Call me Thor and I can muster all the strength that is needed. I have lifted the Midgard serpent causing mother earth to quiver in fear. I am not the strongest, but I can end most with one blow."

"This creature is unlike anything that has been seen before. It leaves no survivors. It is the size of an island, and the threat comes the closer we get to it. There have been whispers that a beautiful goddess has been seen on its shores trying to ward people off but to no avail."

"No survivors? Then I wonder where the whispers came from then," Perseus mentioned while keeping an eye on the threat ahead.

Looking down the telescope, Theseus realised the rumours were true. A beautiful figure of an attractive lady stood on the island frantically waving the three heroes away. This time she wasn't protecting the sailors, she was protecting me. My lady and beloved still cared deeply for me. It goes to show that love is deeper than our outward appearance, good host. It is more magickal than most understand.

Thor unsheathed Mjolnir and raised it high. The dark clouds eclipsed the sun. My tentacles weaved beneath the ocean's surface causing turbulent waters. Their boat rocked violently and the skies rumbled. Thor pulled his hammer back almost placing it on the floor behind him. His weight shifted to his back foot as he twisted and stood side-on. His teeth ground and clenched as he gave every ounce of strength he had to the throw.

At this point, the skies had a deafening roar. My arms reached their boat and climbed up the hull slowly and silently. Perseus and Theseus fought bravely, slicing and stabbing providing Thor enough time. In the blink of an eye, perhaps even quicker, the hammer was launched. Flashes of lightning followed it through the air. The sounds of cracks echoed for miles as Thor unleashed the limits of his strength. Thor roared louder than the rumbling of the thunder. It was like a lion warning others that Midgard was his domain.

Time slowed as the hammer rolled through the droplets of rain. Jord tried to protect me but I was too big to move. She couldn't affect Mjolnir's trajectory because it never misses its target. She simply watched in shock as the incredible force of the blow hit its mark. The loud boom of the impact sent ripples across the ocean sending tsunamis towards villages by the seas. I remember the pain it made me lose the function and control of my tentacles.

The sheer force caused me to rear up and expose my squid-like face. The shriek echoed for kilometres mistaken by those walking the coasts in distant lands as a whistle on the wind. The pain was necessary for my life to end. That is why I sent Thor on his journey. I needed to be set free from this curse. I looked toward my son and smiled at his heroic form holding his mighty weapon. I was proud of all he had overcome in his journey through life. I had helped him in secret, but it took no glory from the accomplishments he had achieved.

As I turned my gaze toward another on the ship all went as planned. Perseus pulled the head of Medusa from his bag. My limbs began to stiffen. They slowly hardened and became more rigid than the roots of Yggdrasil. Gradually they became encased in stone as did the rest of my colossal body. A deceptive island in the vast seas became nothing more than a stone in the ocean.

Jord became furious as her heart broke and the earth trembled in her temper. Seaside villages and kingdoms were swallowed by tsunamis and now exist beneath the currents and waves. The heroes clutched to the ship for dear life. She approached them in the form of a mountain giant. Perseus held up Medusa's head and as the eyes lit up so too did Jord's. She absorbed the magic she used to bargain with Jormungandr in Egypt.

"You took the one I love away from me! And in return you will share his fate!" Her voice boomed intimidatingly.

One by one the heroes were turned to stone. Immortalised in rock and cast back to their homelands. Their images forever inspired heroes throughout time and their characters were explained by the myths and legends they were tied to. As if to encapsulate their legend through time, Jord had allowed their name to live throughout the ages. While I kept a record of their stories to allow other mortals to aspire to such great feats.

Mother earth then turned to Thor and although her heart was broken she was still his mother. Her emotions ran high and her punishment was severe. She took the hammer from his hand and said he was no longer welcome in Asgard. He had to remain with his wife and live like a farmer in solitude. He would tend to the crops in the hope of winning his mother's respect. Tending the land and feeding the mouths of the many, turning the hero into the noble father figure he needed to be.

Every warrior's time ends, good host. We lose our strength and in return, we can only hope to gain wisdom. We must adapt to all that old age brings, and wars never last forever. Years may go by with a multitude of struggles, but it does end if you face them with strength, knowledge, and self-worth then you will survive. Learn from mistakes because strength will return as a form of wisdom. Nothing lasts forever except the name of a good person who has overcome great obstacles under difficult circumstances.

No Time for Heroes

Now comes a darker part of my tale, when the world lost its strength. Loki's mind was as cunning as they come, and his magic and power had no equal. He could exist as a whisper as subtle as the breeze. He could remain out of sight, like a voice in your head. To claim Asgard as his own, he'd have to do three things. The first would be ensuring Thor never came home and he accomplished this by tainting my image. Not only that, but he'd destroy the bond between my son and me.

As Thor wandered back from his sea voyage he became eager to try and change his mother's mind. He considered giving a gift, he played the conversations in his head with words of reason. Unfortunately, when a heart is broken it takes mending first before logic will be heard. Emotional deposits of time listening or shared experiences to build the hope with honour. It will give them something more to hold on to.

Crossing the hills and valleys, Thor came to a large loch. It was way too large to simply walk around so he headed to the pier. It was highly unfortunate that there were no boats to use to cross the massive body of water. Looking outward, in the tranquil nature, all that could be heard were a few bird calls in the distance and the insects chirping. He shielded his eyes from the sun to peer further and he could see that there was an old man fishing.

The old man had a familiar look from a distance. An old weary-looking man with white hair and a grey beard. He wore a wide-brim hat that shaded his eyes covered in darkness. His cloak was a dark shade of grey and his skin was a murky white. In truth, it was his dastardly grin that possibly gave Thor the feeling of familiarity.

"Who is that over in the boat!" Thor called to the fishermen.

"I'm Harbard! And who is the giant idiot by the pier!" The grey-bearded fisherman replied.

"Ferry me over the water and I'll feed you in the morning. I have a basket on my back, no food will be better."

"You praise your food with no idea what lays before you. Word has travelled that your mother may be dead."

Twilight of the Gods: Book of Skuld

"You are conversing with Thor, son of Odin."

"You can call me Harbard because I usually conceal my name. It protects my identity from meeting its doom."

"It would be an unpleasant time to wade to you and wet my prick."

"I'll wait right here for you. You encountered no tougher since Hrungnir's death."

"Your talking of the giant I slew with a head full of stone. He stood once against me but he doesn't stand anymore. Where were you Harbard?"

"I lay with many beautiful witch maidens."

"And how did it go with those women, Harbard?"

"Many types of different women. I even used mighty love spells on witches and charmed them from their men. And where were you, oh mighty Thor?"

"I slew giants in the east. If I hadn't there would be no humans left in Midgard. Where were you Harbard?"

"I was in Valland, and I followed the war. I incited the princes and never reconciled them. Odin owns the nobles who fall in battle and Thor owns the race of thralls."

"Unequally you'd share the glorious dead. If you had as much power as you'd like."

"Thor has enough strength and no heart. Afraid you were a coward that was stuffed in a glove."

The exchange of insults went back and forth for three hours, possibly more. Pointless insults followed by meaningless returns. It was nothing more than boys arguing and trying to be men. In the end, Loki proved the victor as Harbard. He had outwitted Thor and remained far from his strength.

Thor thought his mother was dead and his hammer was lost. Loki's deception was genius. He provoked the hero of Asgard into believing Midgard's elders had lost respect for him or his father didn't want him to return. Both were far from the truth, but because of Loki's talent for lies and deceit, the world lost its greatest hero. The god of heroes, the inspiration for men and women all over. The time of heroes was over, and the world of man was left vulnerable. There was no chance for the little people to prevail against the might of giants. There were no logic defying triumphant victories against monsters. Thor abandoned hope and with it Asgard and Midgard's defence.

Thor had no reason to return to Asgard or aid the lands directly. There would be signs in the skies. Have you ever heard the thunder absent the lightning? Those moments are when he is applying his power against a Jotun. Anything Loki decides to send his way, he will defeat for his fate has already been written but Loki never knew the destiny weaved by Urd, Verdandi and Skuld.

Loki drove a wedge between a kingdom and its mightiest warrior, a father and his son, and a hero against those he was to protect. This marked the beginning of the fall of the gods and the end of the time of heroes. Step by step, Loki's influence on the world was carefully calculated and perfectly executed. He could outwit most of the gods and goddesses of Asgard now, and no one would rise to unite the Germanic tribes against the colossal size of the Roman Empire.

Even in his defeat, Loki still lived to inspire cheaters, liars and leaders to follow his ways. The laws of the world evolved from when only the survival of the strongest applied. People became more intelligent but in doing so strayed from the ways of wisdom and strength. Thucydide once said, "The society that separates its scholars from its warriors will have its thinking done by cowards and its fighting by fools." Children's stories have lost their magical meaning. Leaders became more forked tongued, and nobility has been lost. Judgement was less about your own analysis and more influenced by your peers.

The world is now run by bullies, fools and the greedy. Gold and currency have been given more value than everything that still makes the world magickal. The memories we make, the ancestral lessons and the genetic link that connects us to those throughout the ages. The imagination that inspires creation and creates kinship through common ideas. The aspirations for a better life and the true value of love. That is all that makes the world as we know it magickal. Heroes are created through the challenges we face and the honour we build through the character we have.

The Fall of the Gods

After the time of heroes fell, so too did the magickal world I created alongside my beloved. Loki's dastardly plot had to have a backup just in case I came back to claim my throne one day. After tearing up the bond between father and son, he moved towards my alliance with Hel herself. He could create illusions and manipulate reality to his will. He would make a villain of me but in the times to come he would need his estranged daughter as an ally.

For Loki's plan to succeed, he would have to develop a loving bond between the leader of Asgard and the queen of Niflhel. This relationship would allow death to claim the innocent too. Whether it be through disease, famine or even murder, death itself would give comfort to and rest to everyone that was too young for death. He knew it was the way to provoke and torment my already troubled spirit.

The home of Hel would not only welcome Baldur but keep him from ever leaving. Loki would have to drive a stake into the heart of the alliance between Hel and the Skylands. He would twist its description in the lands of men as a mixture of the cold eeriness of Niflheim and the burning blazes of Muspelheim. Those blazing fires are the habitat of the demons that exist to punish those that hold any memory of Asgard and the glorious gods.

Loki approached his daughter's retreat as I, a grey-bearded wanderer that she believed still ruled the kingdom of the skies. It was a murky swamp with heavy dampness in the air. The unclear waters remained deathly still with no ripples of life existing there. Only the sound of ravens calling from a distance disturbed the deathly silence. Even the air felt thick and heavy in the secluded place.

After Loki got close enough to see her, he remained out of her vision just enough to execute his devious plan. He summoned Hödr, the blind god full of ignorance as a full-fledged warrior and the honourable Honir from Valhöll for a quest of the utmost importance. They both left the comfort of the Skylands to find the Huldra by the dying swamps near Mount Everest. Vegvesir guided them both as it was the sigil Hödr wore to find where he needed to go.

While Loki was disguised as me, Honir and Hödr left to seek out this attractive seductress of the marshes. Her beauty wasn't her only sorcery, she would grant great fortune to those that bed her. This fortune may be a child with great promise or at least a powerful companion in life. She goes by the name of Rind in the land of the living, a name that was inspired by the icy landscapes of Niflheim itself. She enjoyed frolicking in the water and soaking in Sunna's rays by the grassy embankment.

However, rather than leaving her to her own devices, Loki had an even more devious plot to ensure his place of control could not be challenged. Being a leader of gods and men would have bored Loki, he sought only to cause chaos and anarchy. He desired to manoeuvre another to rule the Skylands in his place, a puppet. Easily trusting, easily forgiving and blind to all the crimes humanity would cause.

I have known Hel since she was a little girl. She was well-mannered and behaved respectably despite her unwelcoming treatment when Ullr exiled me. I gave her an entire realm so she would be at comfort and the way the Draugr polluted the world she was the best person for the job. She rules the dead with honour giving them a safe place to rest from a weary life. Old age, hunger, sickness, all these things that cause death were given a reprieve from suffering.

Still secluded from the majority of the outside world, she longed for a companion to share it with. One not intimidated by her true appearance and one that would attempt to brighten her home with their presence. Any strong-willed female leader desires companionship to excel as a leader. Sure, she has performed her role on her own for so long but not having someone to share it with leaves a pretty lonely existence. Time and time again she lay with a variety of mortal men: heroes, villains and even nobles but none lived up to her standards.

Loki approached Hödr and Honir with instructions. They were told to woo her heart and lay with her. During the process, Loki would cast Seidr magic, and she would conceive children for each of them. Honir would be sent first to accomplish this task. He was handsome and noble, everything anyone could want in a partner.

Slowly, he waded through the marshes. As he neared, Loki and Hödr disappeared into the fog. Honir stumbled and slipped aimlessly until he reached the mound where Rind rested. He was dumbfounded by the lady's breathtaking beauty. Her eyes were dark but clear like windows to see your own soul. Her long dark hair fell elegantly down her back. Her curves were subtly enchanting, and her smile distracted you enough to look past her cow's tail.

"Good evening. What brings a good-looking traveller like you to these parts?" Her words dripped softly from her lips.

"My lady, tales have spread to Asgard's halls about your beautiful soul and the rumours of your attractiveness do not do you justice. The nymphs of Alfheim cannot hold a torch that burns like the desire I have for you," Honir declared causing her pale white skin to blush slightly.

"Such kind words from a handsome suitor. You have not come to simply tell me of my beauty, have you?"

Honir shuffled his feet and thought back to stories I shared when charming Gunnlod. "If it is only my words you accept then I shall be happy with the reward of your smile."

"My good honourable god. I wish to share more than my smile with you. Perhaps you should remove your heavy armour and rest a while sharing in each other's warmth."

Honir carefully untied his armour and slowly placed it down not taking his eyes off the beautiful Rind. His heart raced as he approached. Slow pounding beats became more rapid like the war drums of ancient times. The mist became a little thicker concealing their time together from the prying eyes of the others in the swamp. I couldn't do much from death, but I could at least give them their privacy to honour their union.

Despite Loki's lack of vision, Honir's ears could pick up the faint incantation. The Seidr magic he used conceived a child that would later be birthed into the world. Clever Loki always conniving and always plotting. Plan after plan, deception after deception even I found it hard to keep up with him at this point.

Hours passed and Hödr was becoming impatient. "Calm yourself, son. Your time is coming." Loki instructed

Just then, the fog dispersed revealing Rind was alone once more. She lay on the mound content with the time she had shared with Honir. Her eyes smiled as she started towards the skies. Seeing this happiness, Loki became nervous that his scheming had failed once more. Returning Hödr's vision he also created an illusion that disguised the god of cold and darkness. He made him appear as his twin brother, Baldur the beautiful and bold.

Hödr walked towards the beautiful maiden at Loki's instruction. If there was one that could outshine Honir in attractiveness and appeal, it was Baldur. Loki's plot was deceptively brilliant creating a loving attachment to Baldur, so Hel would not return him to Asgard so easily. Wading through the water lighting up the dull swamp with his false glow, Hödr smiled at Rind, which was enough to make her forget her time with Honir.

"But...bu...bu," her tongue was heavy and unable to produce words.

"Hush now, beautiful Rind. I have travelled far and wide just to share a moment or two. Your heart is noble, and I wish to create a stronger union between Asgard and Helheim. If you wish to become queen in the skies as well as queen of the dead, allow me to share some courteous words and delicate touches. Your heart is the only prize I desire, if you would allow me the chance to win it," Hödr spoke boldly.

Rind's speechless and sultry look ran towards Hödr in disguise. Throwing her arms around him she felt the coldness of his skin. Ignoring her gut, she removed his armour and lay with him for hours. Meanwhile, Loki performed Seidr magic once more to conceive the second child in her belly. After all was done, Loki appeared next to the two lovers and lifted the illusion from Hödr. "He he he," Loki laughed, appearing to be me.

"Hödr! You lied to lay with me! Allfather! You cared for me when I was a child and gifted an entire realm to me. Why, why would you do this?"

"You were becoming a threat, little girl. And Asgard does not take kindly to threats."

"You have made a powerful enemy today, Odin. You will regret this on my father's name, you will regret this!"

Rind struggled as much as she could, but Loki's magic was stronger than hers. She was burned by the Seidr magic her mother endured so long ago. Although her fighting spirit far outshone her powerful mother, Loki made her feel weak, and by toying with her heart, poisoned her feeling towards alliance with Asgard and its inhabitants.

Rind's belly began to expand at an alarming rate. She clutched her stomach while she folded over in pain. Screams of anguished echoed to the jaws of Fenrir. The Draugr in Helheim became driven by their queen's anguish. Falling from her womb two children were born as she lay exhausted with blood pouring from her. Returning to her unique form she lay a curse on Hödr.

"Your son will be your end, you liar. Your boy, when he comes of age, will take vengeance for me," she said scornfully.

She then took the other child and transformed each into Lycans, werewolf-like creatures with the ability to harness both wolf-like qualities and human-like behaviours. Honir's child ran into the swamps escaping Loki's control or capture. Hödr's son began snapping at his father but Loki took him to keep Hödr safe.

"Vali, such a violent little pup. I will take you and use you as I need, little one. You remind me of myself in my younger days," Loki stated while staring into the child's eyes.

Hödr and Loki retreated into the mist of the marshes. Hel remained ravaged and bloodied. Once she regained her strength, she became even more withdrawn and hostile to the land of the living. Her heart desired only one that could bring her joy, but for a time she would have to wait.

The two werewolves born were called Vali. One was greedy and the other more reserved. The two wolves mirrored Loki's past, before Gulveig cast her magic on him. Before the war between the Vanir and Aesir. It is funny how things seem to repeat themselves. Slight variances in the evolution of similar stories, but in the end, not many changes regarding the tales we tell.

Under the Mistletoe

There was an uneasy quiet over the realms, but one should never treat quiet as peaceful. Quiet is usually a time when enemies are plotting and trouble approaches. Hel had turned her back on Asgard unknowingly to its leader. Baldur was still drunk from his victory over Loki's direct assault, as were most of the gods. Honir had returned from his travels and even he raised a mead horn to Baldur's glory.

The fires burned and Saehrimnir was sacrificed and served as a glorious feast to celebrate the occasion. Mead horns spilled as loud boasting laughs bellowed throughout the hall. Music was played by Bragi himself to honour the occasion, as he too, took a drink of mortal blood between songs. It was a social gathering the gods had come accustomed to. Celebrating victory and perhaps it was their lack of caution that allowed them to drop their guard once more.

Everyone was gathered in celebration: the elves from Alfheim, the Einherjar wolves of Valhöll and even the dwarves from Svartalfheim came at my Frigg's request. Each had a seat at the table and a plate served with a mead cup full of whatever their taste buds desired. It was a day that not only celebrated the victory but also the acknowledgement of Baldur's rise to Hlidskjalf. However, sometimes the days we celebrate, no matter the victory, leave us complacent to those that will try and bring us down.

These celebrations lasted for three whole days and three beautiful nights. On the first day of festivities, Loki approached the hall in disguise. He mingled with everyone subtly probing for information to put another wedge between Asgard and the other realms. If more realms turned on Asgard the world would descend further into chaos. Landvættir would be less peaceful towards the inhabitants of Midgard and begin tormenting even those that are undeserving of punishment.

On the second day, Loki approached his mother, not as himself but as Lofn. Frigg was still a broken woman with a shattered heart. The gold tears had dried, but her eyes lost their sparkle. Gnoss and Gersemi shone no more and the smile on her face fell from its glory. Her only happiness was seeing her beautiful boy, Baldur, ascend as the ruler of Asgard. Pride and joy came knowing that Asgard's successor was more than worthy to hold the position.

"My queen, tell me everything about our king-to-be. I'd like to admire and understand all that he's endured in his many heroic endeavours," Loki enquired.

"To talk of Baldur distracts me from my grief. Which tale would you like to hear, my dear Lofn?"

"My queen I'd love to hear of his tale against Fafnir. A dragon and a knight, those kinds of stories always make me swoon with excitement and awe."

Frigg proceeded to tell the magnificent tale, beautifully. No detail was missed and no word of a lie. It sparked wonder and awe in Loki's mind. He was silent and although he'd never admit it, he was impressed. Each detail shared was ammunition for Loki to prod at Baldur's seemingly impenetrable armour. However, Loki's mind was the most versatile and cunning. He continued his portrayal of innocence while asking for more information.

"That helmet he had was certainly impressive. Did it really have an oath from everything? Is Baldur truly invulnerable?" Loki asked.

"There was one thing, that missed taking the oath, Lofn."

"No, really? What and why?"

"A small plant that sprang from the end of the Hreidmir line. The dwarven blood mixed after Regin and Fafnir fell to Baldur's blade. Its name is mistletoe."

"Ah, such a small weed. It couldn't harm Baldur anyway. You weren't to know, Allmother. It was only created after the fact. I'm sure a small thing can't hurt someone as beautiful and bold as Baldur..."

"Fate can't be changed my dear Lofn. Another also never swore the oath of harming Baldur."

"Really! Do tell."

"His brother, Hödr. They balance each other but complement each other too. Innocence and ignorance allow a world full of wonder and awe where the possibilities seem endless. Baldur will die and dark times will follow. Such is the way of life, my friend."

"Don't speak of such things, my queen. May we enjoy Baldur's rule for many years to come," Loki said faking sincerity. "I must go and prepare for the entertainment tomorrow. It is always fun testing Baldur's invulnerability. He's almost perfect, so dreamy."

Loki left with the information needed. Now his devious plot would require his ally, Hödr. His darkness brought balance to the light that shone from Baldur. His coldness tempered the warmth from his glorious brother. It was a prediction Urd made so long ago. Brother would kill brother in the early signs of Ragnarok. Loki would manipulate Hödr into his devious plot, just to remove any threat that Loki considered Asgard could bring to him spreading chaos. Hödr would be his puppet from a position of power.

Loki travelled to the site where Fafnir was slain. The ground was no longer stained with blood and even the bones fertilised the growth of the unique plant. It was green with small white berries mixed amongst its foliage. It was small and dainty, and it didn't take much to turn what appeared harmless to many into a weakness of one.

Loki plucked the small plant that sprouted from Hreidmir's bloodline and took it to Fjalar, the last of the Strigoi craftsmen. Only someone of great skill at creating magickal gifts could make a weapon from something so delicate, and something so innocent. With the power of unlimited imagination and Verdandi's powers to bring the impossible into reality with creativity, he could make almost anything. With a love of his craft and inspiration from memories past, his weapon would aspire to become a legend. The Hreidmir line was his ancestors, and even in their death, they aided in the creation of something that would change the future. He honoured his genetic link to the past, as he was the last of the kin remaining left.

Fjalar was reluctant to help Loki at first, but Loki had Verdandi's power now. He would live in fear of Loki's power and bend to his will simply to avoid punishment or torture. Another reason why characters like Loki should not rule. They abuse their power simply to keep others beneath them and in turn lose the honour of leadership. Leadership belongs to those that help others surpass themselves regardless of power and control.

After Loki received the arrow, he returned to Asgard to complete his plan. He could move much more swifty now, teleporting to wherever he needed to be in an instant. He could slip into shadows or exist on the breeze, as his power came with so much freedom it poisoned his spirit further. He truly was all-powerful but until Baldur was removed, he would never be truly free.

The gods continued to rejoice in Loki's defeat, and this infuriated the trickster further. As stealthy as a mosquito on a hot summer's day, Loki placed the arrow in Hödr's quiver. However, he couldn't leave such an influential part of the plan to chance. He slipped deeper in disguise and became a voice in Hödr's head, a devil on his shoulder, if you will. Loki masked his voice as mine and guided Hödr's actions and thoughts. Not a single god or goddess could see or hear Loki. Even Hödr was ignorant of the trickery and deception. Hödr believed it was my ghost guiding him to claim the throne. After all this time I trained him first not Baldur.

The sun was at its highest of the day and all were gathered at the arena to celebrate. The cheers were deafening as Baldur entered the arena. He raised his arms to accept the praise and cheers, but as he lowered his arms, the viewers fell into silence. He stood in the centre unafraid. His confident smile was only outdone by his outstretched arms calling forth the challenge. A series of gods entered the arena dawning all kinds of weapons.

A booming laugh echoed throughout the Skylands as he antagonised the crowd into an uproar. He laughed foolishly confident in his invulnerability. One should never taunt fate because, in the end, nothing lasts forever, good host. It appeared nothing could harm him. Blades became blunt as they tried to sever his limbs. Rocks bounced from his chest at every attempt and spears never pierced flesh. My Frigg pulled Mjolnir from her purse and spoke to the crowd sending their jaws lower in awe.

"We all know the legend tied to this mighty weapon. Any foe it has faced has never outlived one blow from the greatest hammer ever made. The lightning cracks with every blow made by such a weapon. Let us see if Baldur is truly the greatest choice to rule."

As she released the hammer, Baldur's face showed signs of concern. It flew swiftly as time began to slow. It never missed its target. The crowd watched in disbelief and terror as it launched towards their king. Despite the thousands of great Jotun that the hammer had slew before, when it hit Baldur, it never made a mark. It returned to Frigg's hand and the crowd erupted. It was due to the Allmother's efforts so long ago to protect her beautiful boy. Not even the legendary hammer of the thunder god could affect Baldur's awe-enchanting form.

Suddenly, darkness fell across the arena as a familiar challenger appeared. The temperature dropped and breath became steam. Hödr wandered slowly from his seat in the arena. Loki had been picking at his mind for hours now. Taunting him, ridiculing him to act against his brother. Dull whispers became loud echoing screams in Hödr's head. Loki was relentlessly giving him only one way out. Test his brother's immortality to make the voice stop.

"It isn't fair everyone else gets to take part. Maybe if you just have a little attempt, what could it hurt?"

The crowd roared in laughter, taunting Hödr further. It dulled to a cold silence as Hödr took his place. He reached behind himself searching his quiver for the perfect arrow. In his head, Loki guided him to the one made from mistletoe. "Not that one, or that one. Yes, that is the perfect arrow," Loki whispered in Hödr's head. He drew his bow and Loki guided his shot. "Higher and a little to the left," Loki whispered further.

Baldur's confidence grew as he raised his hands out wide. He taunted the crowd's cheer as Hödr readied his attempt. The wind was light as time slowed. Hödr drew a deep breath as he pulled the bowstring back. The air was dry and Hödr's tasted the dust in the arena. An entire moment felt like a lifetime as the arrow was released and set to purpose. It flew the air swift and true, straight to the heart of innocence.

Baldur felt pain and saw his blood for the first time since his ascension to Asgard. He looked down at the arrow gasping for air as his blood filled his lungs. His glow faded and his smile fell. He plucked the arrow made from mistletoe from his chest. His blood stained the sand beneath as the celebrations fell to silence. As Baldur dropped to his knees, no longer breathing, the crowd's silence became gasps and loud screaming. Frigg dropped to her knees and the skies wept to flood the lands below.

A sad time had come to pass in the world, where Baldur was no longer in the land of the living or existed in the realm of the gods. The world had lost its wonder and glow, and although life remained, it all seemed a little duller than before. Asgard had no king, and they were weakened by the grief of such a catastrophe. Even Hödr wept for his brother as he did not wish him dead.

Loki stealthily departed Hödr's head so he could influence what would come next. His plot was calculated and as intricate as they come, and each plot was a victory that won the heart of Tyr's wife. Each success inspired her lustful heart to Loki's side, and if he could get one over the brave god of war, then even better in his mind. His scheme was not yet over, but he was one step closer to defeating the gods and claiming Asgard as his own.

And now you know the reason we kiss under the mistletoe at Yule, good host. It is to show our love and respect for the memory of the fallen one. To honour and remember Baldur in his death because nothing lasts forever, good host. However, a tradition tied to beauty and innocence, sealed with a kiss ensures the name of a great one lives beyond death. Traditions keep the old ways alive, hidden amongst seasons and mythology. Respect the honourable dead.

Regaining Your Innocence

Most things, once they are gone, are never truly regained in the same version as before. Although our ignorance takes most things away, we should not rely on it to think things can go back to the way they were. Only the wise appreciate what they have before losing it. It takes great insight, perceptual understanding and awareness to be truly grateful for something you have yet to lose.

Baldur was dead and the world has lost its wondrous shine. It had changed everything. Children no longer believed in the magic that stories and tales brought. The limitless power of imagination had been polluted with intelligence and ignorance. Those that dared to dream and believe in mysticism beyond what they knew as reality were mocked and ridiculed. The world was colder and darker because Hödr was ignorant of Loki's aid.

The gods gathered in Midgard as they paid their final respects to Baldur. Everyone's eyes were wet as their hearts were heavy with grief. It was quiet with only the sounds of weeping to fill the silence.

The gods mourned for nine days and nights before action and decision were taken. Nanna begged and pleaded with what she believed to be me for a solution. Unfortunately, it was Loki, and he had no intention to return Baldur to the world. He desired to place a puppet on the throne of Asgard while he continued as he pleased unchallenged and not controlled.

"As hard as it is to lose another brother, Hödr should be killed for the death of Baldur!" Tyr demanded.

"Death is severe for an accident. Can't we forgive and forget? I can't kill my own child, without first giving him a chance to correct his error," Loki responded, keeping up appearances.

"There is freedom in forgiveness but to forget would leave you open for another transgression. How can Hödr fix it, he can't go to Helheim and bring Baldur back, can he?" Freyr asked.

"Perhaps he can. If he takes the sleigh and Prancer, he could go to Helheim and demand his return. She was gifted a realm of her own so long ago. Maybe she'll allow the Aesir this special request," Loki suggested.

"No-one can tame the Kelpie other than you, Odin. It may be in our favour if you go to ask. Hel may honour your gift with another and return Baldur to us," Nanna's voice whimpered through the grief of her lost love.

"I am not here to right the wrongs of another. I am here to suggest a solution that won't result in the death of another god. Hödr may ride Sleipnir to Helheim deep in the heart of the beast. I will grant him the use of my chariot and steed."

"Please Allfather!"

"Enough! I am not your saviour! I have nine realms to watch over! Do not ask me again!" Loki's voice boomed sending Nanna retreating with only Forsetti to hold and her tears for comfort.

Hödr was fetched and placed in front of Loki and the council of gods. Even the wind held his breath as the tension rose. Valhöll fell into silence as Hödr stood in the centre awaiting a verdict. The onlooker's stern looks pierced his armour. The golden tears of Mother Frigg began falling once again. If she was to suffer another child lost, she would turn her back on the world and Asgard. A recluse, a goddess reduced to the level of a witch vilified by the Christian belief Loki created with Rome.

Loki loved tormenting his mother. The gold her tears produced could be used with the mortals but first, he had to exile the gods from the Skylands and claim his freedom. A dog without a master, Loki became soulless and indifferent to everyone and anyone he wished to torment. He was greed personified and with the ability to be satisfied his appetite for chaos grew further.

"Hödr, do you know why you have been summoned here?" Loki asked sternly, with his two wolves growling by his side.

"My brother's death, father."

"Yes, you must seek out Hel and beg for Baldur's release. When Baldur is feasting in Valhöll as part of the Einherjar, then forgiveness will be yours."

"For now, I will go by Hermod as I go searching for my brother's soul. I will use every ounce of my warrior spirit until the task is complete," Hödr firmly requested.

"Seek out my horse, the eight-legged one by the water. It shall take you deep into the heart of Helheim. Into the jaws of Fenrir and beyond the realm of the living. You will be living and unwelcome so spend as little time as you can there."

Loki knew me well enough to create little suspicion. My mannerisms, my verbal delivery and how I presented myself. He fooled every god, elf and even the warrior werewolves in my hall. They followed his rule without question. It seemed that his little trick was executed with impressive accuracy. As a side effect of assuming my form, the people of Midgard began to vilify me. Convinced I was more of a malevolent god known as Fimbultyr.

Hödr left my hall and walked towards the dark shadowy waterhole where the clouds became mist. There was a damp smell in the air as the sun's brightness faded. Haunting neighs drifted from beyond the fog as ripples crept up onto the edge of the water. Bones of foolish elves and ignorant dwarves were scattered on the embankment. A warning to the living from those that were unlucky enough to fall prey to the Kelpie's charm. Its beauty could even seduce the blind into danger.

As the horse's neighs became more prominent, the sound of splashes could be heard inbetween. Heavy hard steps in the water became light splashes as the dark silhouette appeared in the middle of the lake. Its shape was as fluid as a shadow moving under the gloomiest light. It was truly terrifying and only I could master its temperament.

Suddenly, the shape and sound disappeared from vision. Hermod stumbled back until he felt something large at his back. A cold shiver went up his spine as the air became colder. As he turned, he was confronted by the fiery death horse. Its fur was as black as the night itself, but Hermod had to save his brother. He climbed my steed bravely and set to his purpose.

It reared and neighed so loud that the haunting sound could be heard throughout the realm of Asgard. Some legends tell of a pumpkin-headed rider through Midgard, claiming souls on their way to the realm of the dead. Paying a toll to enter the jaws of death, passed the teeth of the behemoth and into the belly of the beast. However, the gods of one religion become the demons of another.

The sleigh slid behind the Kelpie through the sky with quick haste. Overland, it was still faster than anything ever seen in the realms. Overwater, it slipped over the surface on its skis. With the mighty steed, formally known as Svadilfari, the sleigh was still the magnificent wonder that inspires tales of me to this day.

Hermod swiftly crossed the veil between the land of living and dead. The realm was cold and dark, hidden in Niflheim. Although the gate was in Nepal the realm of the dead was concealed in Antarctica. Ice and snow reminded me of the time before Ymir was slain. My time in the realm was a reminder that I still had much to do, and my oath on my spear allowed me to come and go for years to come.

I managed to make my way through the Draugr to deliver advice to my son. I told him to mask himself in death to make his journey easier. The Draugr would not suffer the living, even a god was unwelcome. I gave him a black rock, a lump of coal because if all else failed the fire would keep the dead at safe distance.

Hermod and Prancer galloped toward the heart of Helheim. He was escorted by the undead servants and seated at their queen's table. Hel wasn't present yet, she was busy feeding Nidhoggr and sending fire Jotun to Muspelheim for Surtr's army. Loki had already destroyed ties between Helheim and Asgard but what he did to Hel was so much worse.

Loki not only allowed the rape of his daughter, but he also aided it. He chose his target well. Hödr was the intended target for his plot. Sending him to Hel would provoke her to not grant favour to his brother's return. Hödr took his seat waiting patiently for the queen of the Draugr to host his request.

The large door to her hall creaked and groaned as Hel entered. A deathly silence followed her around the room as she floated to her chair. As she sat the tension became thick although her half-decayed face remained unchanged. Her beautiful side wept as she recognised her previous attacker.

"What name do you go by living one? What brings you here? Why have you come to my domain?"

"I am Hermod and I have come to beg you for Baldur's return to Asgard."

"You lie! You thought I would not recall all you made me endure? What is your real name, foolish god?"

"I'm Hödr and I have never encountered you before, Queen of the Draugr."

"Do you not recall the mound? Do you not recall a maiden called Rind?"

"I do but that was not you...was it?"

"It was you fool, and you should never treat a maiden in such a way. You and your father have no honour. You may have Baldur..."

"Thank you, your highness."

"Let me finish fool! You may have Baldur if you can get everyone across the nine realms to weep for him. Every animal, every insect, every Jotun, and elf. Every dead person and those that remain alive. All must weep for Baldur for his return to Valhöll."

Höd's mind was burdened by the scale of such a request. He left and for nine days and nine nights he scoured the lands on my Kelpie. The eight legs trampled over land and water with great haste. Unknown to all my spirit snuck out of Helheim with him. I was free from death and now my soul could be reincarnated just as my oath declared.

He gathered tears from the entire world. Everyone wept for Baldur and shed a tear to commemorate his passing. Each elf, dark elf, human and god all wept for Baldur. Every animal, insect and even Jotun mourned for Baldur's return. Everything looked to be in Asgard's favour until Hermod reached Tokk.

Not all was as it appeared with the Jotun. She was a witch that lived in seclusion from even the rest of her kind. An odd little cabin by a river with doors to the north, east, south, and west. A little house so she can come and go in any direction she chooses. The home was quant by a beautiful stream. The salmon frolicked in the water with a fishing pole perched in place. All appeared tranquil and at peace.

Hermod cleared his throat before humbly requesting her donation of tears. She refused his request abruptly. She said, "I will weep waterless tears for Baldur's fate. Living or dead I never cared for this son of Odin. Let Hel keep what she has."

Hermod's chance failed, so close to the finish line. His failure would result in his execution, but he faced his fate unafraid of the consequences. He began showing his nobility and I couldn't have been prouder. However, the ways of old are clear a death for a death and the death of Baldur would not be forgotten.

Baldur would remain by Hel's side as a companion ruling over the dead in Helheim. Höd failed to reclaim his brother for Asgard but Loki wasn't finished with him. Loki was behind Höd's failure. He disguised himself as Tokk and refused Baldur's return. He required Baldur to remain out of the picture. For if he came back then Asgard would forever remain beyond Loki's manipulation.

Loki's plan was in three parts. Tearing Asgard and Helheim's allegiance apart; indirectly killing Baldur and removing him from life and the kingdom of Asgard; the final part was ensuring he stayed dead. Now that his main competition was gone, he would now have to find a way to disband the gods forcing them into hiding. He would do this by faking grief and scattering them to the four winds.

Not all was lost for Loki through this victory over the gods he gained a companion in Sigyn, Tyr's former wife. He also gained two sons. Hödr would now be known as Narfi and to keep him safe from his fate, Vali Hödrson would become his lap dog. Honir left with his child, also known as Vali, to live a life filled with honour and duty.

The Spirit of Yule is Lost

You might be thinking, "why didn't I stick around to stop it?" I mean I knew it was coming because it had been scripted by the Nornir so long ago. The power of fate is not to be cursed, some are born luckier than others, and this should not cause hate in retaliation. Wisdom, honour and respect is the prize for those that accept their control over what happens between birth and death. To live cautiously may bring you peace but respect will only be gained from a few.

The sun rose on a new day, but its glow had faded somewhat from the world. The clouds became dreary and grey. Sadness gripped the heart of Yggdrasil through the power of intelligence and ignorance. The joys were not as glorious as before and the magickal world we exist in had lost its wonder and awe. The greatness achieved was not as great as it once was, and the wonders of myths and folklore were dismissed as superstition and overactive imaginations.

Hödr returned to Asgard to face the gods' judgement. He was the cause of the world to shine a little less. He caused the world to become a little colder and a little darker. To his surprise, Asgard was vacant of elves, gods and Jotuns. The Valkyrie flew amongst the clouds and the Einherjar continued their training, but the gods were not there to sentence Hödr.

After searching the Skylands, Hödr marched to Valhöll to seek answers from his father. He used his might to open the heavy doors but what greeted him was a figure of wicked nature and cunning tongue. "Loki? What are you doing here?"

"Great Hödr, I have come to give you an offer. One which to refuse will make you the greatest fool of all," Loki grinned.

"Where is Odin? Where is my father? Where are the gods?"

"He...is no longer, mighty Odinson. Odin is dead, killed by Thor."

"Thor wouldn't kill Odin, fool!"

"No, but he would kill a monster, especially one that existed at sea."

"True but what does that have to do with my father?"

"A little trickery, a little shapeshifting and manipulation because there are no limits to my power."

"So, who is in charge of the Skylands?"

"That is my proposition to you, dear Hödr. Become the God of the skies, the only god and all under you will love you as they did Baldur. Take the name of Fimbultyr and swear your allegiance to me and you will have it all."

Although much had changed since Hödr was known as Geirrod, an offer like that would make anyone regress to their old ways. I mean Hödr would become as great as his beloved brother. He would be respected, loved, and praised even in his absence, a blind faith if you will. It was Loki's final step toward his freedom. Freedom to toy with and torture mortals, freedom to provoke the Jotun race and the freedom to fade other beliefs and traditions away from the world.

"I accept Loki! I thought I'd be sentenced to death for my involvement in Baldur's death. This has been quite a turnaround."

"You would have nothing if it wasn't for me. All hail Narfi! All hail the God almighty!"

Meanwhile, the funeral proceedings continued on a miserable day in Midgard. It was a funeral like no other. It would be the grandest gesture anyone would receive in death from now until Ragnarök. The skies wept a drizzle of tears as the grey clouds made the day a little gloomier. The world wept for his passing: every Jotun, elf and god shed their tears at the sadness that had come to the realms.

All that wished to be there gathered at Shieldaig on the coast of Scotland. The dark elves and dwarves, the Jotuns and Vanir, and the elves and gods all gathered to say farewell. Freyr pulled his scarf from his bag. He began unfolding the cloth as his armour Gullinbursti glow faded a little. With each unfold of the cloth his great ship appeared. He gifted Skidbladnir to the fallen Baldur so he might float with favourable winds to his final place of rest.

Freyr's ship was so colossal it seemed as if an entire Island unfolded before them. The boat would put Noah's mythical Arc to shame. The sheer size of the ship would require a strength unrivalled in all the realms. The gods collectively tried to move it with all their might, but it didn't budge, not even a millimetre. My beloved Jord wept harder because her beautiful boy could not receive his proper send-off. He would not exist amongst the freedom of the ocean. He would not remain subtly in the waves of thought the humans have.

The gods sent for Thor's aid to move the ship. A few moments later the grey gloomy clouds grumbled as he approached on his chariot pulled by his two powerful goats. He came out of honour for his fallen brother, but he knew he was not welcome. His mother took his hammer from him, and Loki's masquerade made him feel that even I did not want to endure his company.

Frigg turned away and refused to even lay eyes on him, never mind speak to him. The grief of loss shook her to the core. She secluded herself from the rest of the gods and even her legend and love would fade from the earth. For the love of earth had lost its innocence and even the knowledge of her was now gone from the minds of the descendants of Askr and Embla.

Thor approached the ship confidently from the rear and planted his feet firmly in the sand on the shore. He tightened Megingjord and spat on the grips of his iron gauntlets. He squatted low scooping the bottom of the ark. He grunted and heaved as he extended his legs, but the boat did not rise. Thor's legs extended but the weight of the vessel cause his legs to go deeper into the sand. The gods were dumbfounded without a proper solution, Baldur's body would remain on the shores of Scotland.

Suddenly, Loki appeared still like me and smirked at Thor's failure. "Even the so-called mighty Thor cannot honour his brother's memory by aiding in a proper send-off, pfft." A small dwarf began sniggering next to Thor. Soon those subtle laughs became louder and more prominent. Thor became infuriated by the disrespect and kicked the dwarf launching him into the air. The dwarf must have flown nine kilometres before landing with a sore bum and a bruised ego.

Loki knew of one much stronger than Thor. The only Jotun known to defeat the hero of Asgard. Loki sent for Skadi, the one who single-handedly managed to defeat Thor, and Tyr and even caused Odin to bargain with her for peace. Loki was reluctant as she had caused him much pain and discomfort, but the sooner Baldur was not the focus, he could get on with creating chaos and discomfort in the realms.

Skadi came from the mountains in Scandinavia upon her giant wolf that she rode as most others would ride horses. She began her approach as her heart felt heavy at the loss of the one she desired so long ago. The gods stood back in awe as her Jotun steps shook the world. Although her eyes welled, she stood confident in her abilities to send Baldur off to his resting place. With one powerful push, the boat cut through the sand like a hot knife through butter.

Thor withdrew from his failed attempt and retreated amongst the crowd. The mighty thunderer huffed because of the shame he felt as a cast out and the ridicule he endured from his once-beloved father. His heroic character had been conquered by her before. He was supposed to be the strength of the gods, he was the one they called upon when no one else was able to complete a task. This shame forced him into the background and his victories faded from the minds of those who once belonged to Asgard.

"Stop wench! I have something to gift Baldur before he is placed to rest."

"Allfather, I know you are grieving but you have always welcomed me before. Why such disrespect?"

"Silence! You are beneath me. Wait here I may decide to answer you after I gift Baldur something," Loki snarled.

The gods looked at Loki as they lost respect for me as a king and a ruler. His actions and words were not worthy of someone on the throne. Some may justify it with suffering but there is no excuse to treat others badly. We are how we act in the present moment. Even though it wasn't me, the gods perceived it as me because Loki's disguise was very convincing. Loki climbed onto the boat and leaned over to Baldur's ear.

"It was I who killed you. It was Loki. You may have been protected by our mother but no one in the nine realms can outsmart me. Take Draupnir. I pulled it from your father's body before I turned him into a sea creature. In time, the weight of Draupnir will sink you to the ocean depths."

Loki placed my arm ring Draupnir on the corpse's chest while covering his sinister grin. As he departed from the ark, so the grin on his face left. His posture hunched over to the old man he was pretending to be. Slowly hobbling from the massive boat, he shoulder-barged Skadi on his way past.

"Ok now you may push the ship wench," Loki growled disrespectfully.

Skadi ground her teeth and mumbled under her breath. Her wolves snarled at the imposter as Vali growled back. With one mighty push, Skadi launched the mighty ship. The sand parted as the waves did. It was as if Skadi and Njörd worked together despite their differences.

Skinbladnir drifted peacefully off, carried by the wave maidens. As soon as the large vessel got a little off the shore, my Frigg used her earth magic to change the boat to a small island. It was a beautiful land with fairy pools and a rocky mountainscape that symbolised my approval of his rise as king. The Storr was a thumbs up to my selected successor. The isle of Skye was her way of keeping father and son together.

Skadi mounted her large wolf. Each step they took could be heard through the forests and the howls almost haunted the nights in Scandinavia. They were like cries out to Mani for comfort in the darkness. Sobbing for the one lost, the one that sails on the sky boat, the one that was the light of life. Baldur the fallen king of the Skylands.

Terrible tales travelled in the lands of Midgard of a monstrous witch and terrifying werewolves. Loki's religion vilified Skadi and any other people who kept the belief in animism. She was powerful and skilled enough to outmanoeuvre and outwit any mortal of Midgard. No mortal army or hunter could ever defeat a god or goddess.

The gods turned their back, not only on the corpse of Baldur but on Asgard itself. Each of them retreated to their lands vowing never to answer Odin's call again. Loki had dissolved the kinship the gods had by vilifying their leader, me. All the gods decided to live in solitude far from humans, Jotuns and godly obligations. The realms were more apart than ever although sometimes you would hear tales of strange creatures or hallucinations of humans when they spotted a Jotun or Aesir.

Tyr left to live in solitude in Jotunheim because his wife left him for Loki. She was driven by her desire for victory and Loki's victory over the gods was complete. He now was left to live freely. None could control and none could threaten him. He could toy with and spread chaos throughout the lands. Loki ruled as a false God, Jesus was Hödr and he maintained the Skylands. He used many names in many countries and kingdoms. He was Allah, Abraham, the Lord almighty and as long as his followers venerated him, as his greedy ego would be kept at bay.

His next step was to turn the Valkyrie into angels. They would be his soldiers against any Jotun attack. The Einherjar would be his elite assassins sent on hunting missions to seek out and cause the gods to keep hiding and evolving to mask their identity from the humans. The werewolves would inspire his worshippers to seek out all pagan followers, anyone even thinking about keeping traditions and beliefs alive. If there were any whispers of Odin or Thor or any other god or goddess not in his service, they would be hunted without mercy.

The world was darker now, but an oath made on an enchanted spear ensured that Loki would not rule unopposed. I would return from death as a mortal. Time and time again to wither Loki's authority over the world of man. The key to defeating lies and deception is truth and knowledge. However, I can't fully defeat Loki in a mortal form, I'd have to find a way to regain a power equal to his. I needed to restore the kinship of the gods. I would need to educate the world and why it remains magickal.

The Ghost of Christmas Past

I have lived a thousand lifetimes, possibly more. My mind is full of families created, people inspired, and lives fulfilled. You'll have heard of me in the myths and possibly in the history books. I have been men, women, and children throughout the ages. You will have heard whispers and some shocking tales, and all are true. For the world, I love I have done some heinous and beautiful things while enduring mortality.

I have existed behind the scenes, constructing wars and massacres stretching throughout the world. I gave a poor man enough dowry for his three daughters to be wed. I have gifted coal to those in need of warmth during the coldest of winter nights. I have fought the demonic Krampus that tormented the innocent. I went by many names as a god but even more in my mortal lives. I was a saint when I was Nicholas. I have led armies to glory. I was even a mage as Sinterklaas, but I'll tell you that tale another time. Allow me to explain why I caused so much death, not for forgiveness but for understanding. It was all for the one I love.

How do you charm the earth, mother nature herself, good host? You reduce the burdens she endures. With life exponentially expanding to accommodate the ever-rising population, the earth requires a reprieve. Too much life will always equate to death, so the balance must be maintained.

Humans have become the problem. Most species of creatures adapt to their surroundings but on the other hand, humans use their technology to shape the world around them. More people mean more animal breeding programs for food. This in turn creates laziness, due to the convenience of the availability of sustenance. Survival is not a prize for the brave and evolved, it is now a luxury overlooked. Illness, injury, and health have been enhanced through the science of medicine allowing the population to grow further out of control.

Although humans are intelligent creatures, they have become easy to manipulate. A word here, a whisper there, each perfectly placed at the right moment guaranteed death and war. Desires and focus on hardship is the easiest thing to manipulate. Greed is what humanity has come accustomed to. Riches, sex and self-elevation drive humans and their selfish needs. Emotions run high when control is taken, and the ego is challenged, leaving war as the only answer.

Whether it is power, land or fossil fuels, war is the easiest option for those that are fuelled by greed. Financial, biological or any other tools used to fuel conflict, humans are the easiest to influence. Whether I was the wife of a king or an advisor to a general, it was always easy to provoke a thought towards a fight. Reducing the population of the world by a couple of hundred thousand at a time would fertilize the soil with blood and bone and my Frigg would thrive a little better than before. After all, I vowed to ease her burdens on our wedding day.

My many names as a father figure around Yule were the other side of my charm. Father Christmas, Santa Claus, and the wild huntsman are only some of the titles I go by in the latter part of the year. You may be wondering why, good host. Well, my wife is also a goddess of love and motherhood. Therefore, as a good husband reducing her burdens, I also wish to warm her cold heart by bringing joy to the children of the world.

There are a few things left to wonder about when it comes to characters. We assume to know all but only a fool boasts of his knowledge. When seated with the wise you will be humbled or forever remain the fool. Creating magic and awe is one of the few things that can even outdo religious control. Stories and songs surrounding myths and traditions kept the old ways alive.

Its title may be Christmas, but Yuletide carols and the gifting cycle is of Pagan origins. Easter may have been twisted by Loki into a resurrection, but the bunny was I, and the fertility goddess was my lady. Halloween was a time to tribute to all the wonderful and magical creatures and even the dead could exist in the world amongst the living. Even the inspiration for the tooth fairy was my doing when I gifted Lord Cernunnos or Freyr a realm of elves and fairies when he cracked his first tooth. All these traditions and myths do not link up with current religious practice but instead, show that people still wish to believe in something more.

People may be ignorant of the meanings but whether they look deeper for knowledge inside myths or take them for face value the old ways still transcend a time when Loki irradicated all other beliefs and practices. I wrote the Bible with the runes I learned hanging on the tree. The Pagan stories with biblical twists and name changes but also plot holes big enough to make deep thinkers question beliefs. Subtle enough to escape Loki's view but the hints are there.

In the book of Enoch, God created the Leviathan, the great sea serpent and even the Behemoth. These two creatures share an awful likeness to the Midgard serpent and Fenris wolf that will destroy my life. As long as Loki's ego was stroked with glory and victory, he allowed it to remain in his book. Noah's ark and the world flooding were inspired by Bergelmir and his wife's survival establishing Jotunheim. Satan's more popular mythic description is based on Surtr's awesome and terrifying form in Muspelheim. These tales are there if you can only see with more than just your eyes.

My first life as a mortal was as King Solomon. I used what I had learned when creating the Hávamál to host enemies and respectfully collect knowledge without them becoming aware. As long as I mentioned "God" they left without disruption. It was due to Loki's pact with Hödr. Knowledge is power, good host. It is better to question two opposing perspectives so that we can establish our own. I met with a demon prince, a lord of Jotuns that had been imbued with terrible power thanks to Loki's new gifts. He gave me respect and with his aid, I hosted several demons in my castle.

A gift for a gift, they shared their stories, and I returned with the courtesy of not using my magic to trap them. I questioned each demon I hosted in my hall to discover their purpose in the world. Each demon and spirit informed me of their powers, but after a while they also revealed their weaknesses. Curses and tortures they would unleash in the world would keep the population controlled for a time. It kept me from causing so much global war and devastation and allowed me to focus on returning the world to its magickal roots.

For the sake of Loki, I twisted Solomon's story and character to fit his support of Hödr's rule. To remove suspicion from my existence, I used the phrase, "with the power of God," in the testament I wrote. However, after it hinted that it was my character under a different name, he removed the tale from the book. It was a religious takeover and trying to control the world is a battle of wit and half-truths. Although Loki had strength in numbers and the power of Verdandi, I could outwit him during his rise. A name change, but the bones of pagan myths existing beneath the surface, was my greatest deception of all.

That is the power of the runes, good host. With letters, you can conjure a word. With words, you can create a sentence. With sentences, you can cultivate paragraphs. With paragraphs, you can manifest chapters, and with chapters, you can enchant a story. The wisdom of the runes is letter by letter, word by word the building blocks of storytelling.

I used to be a sorcerer, but this magic was far superior to any godly enchantments that came before. As a god, I've created the world and those that inhabit it. As a human, I have created many worlds and many more tales that create wonder and awe. Whispers, myths, and superstitions all have you questioning reality. Whether it was a bigfoot sighting, or the Loch ness monster that was spotted, it has most wondering if there is more to the world than we think we know.

The second magic I gained as a god was the mead of poetry and I have used that in combination with the Runes. Creating an emotional connection to a saga means the story doesn't just stay in your mind but also in your heart. Rhythm and Rhyme and writing techniques take you on a journey of the mind. Creating a world or creature that has never been seen before. The world, my beloved lady, is still M.A.G.I.C.K.A.L, good host.

Memories

Muninn is magickal and a key to a few
Doors that are locked to stories that are new.

Memories are lessons, a wisdom that is true
To guide your journey towards something new

Memories give direction whether they're yours or someone you knew
A Vegvesir compass to reach a path that is for few

Before you take a step on the path that you choose
Remember failure is certain but it doesn't mean you lose

No path is easy, that's the unfortunate truth
But remember why you started and some woes will be soothed

So remember good host memories are magickal
The good, the bad and especially the radical

Ancestors

When there are times you feel all alone
Remember your story is not yours to own

The paths you wander, the mountains you roam
The foundations were set by Urd so long ago

Stories and whispers as old as the stones
We are where we are now through blood spilt and buried bones

Freedoms were won battles were lost
The past can be as bitter as Niflheim's frost

Regardless of what they did, they did it for you
An ancestor's story is as delicate as dew

So remember good host when you start something new
Your ancestors gave you a chance for all that you do

Genetics

Genetics is a link to those from the past
And those in the future, life goes pretty fast

Strands of code called DNA
A twisted ladder into the fray

Even if you look to a moment in time
Your roots run deeper so keep that in mind

Askr and Embla started us all
ignorance of that means the world will fall

Your mother and your father, parts you can't pick
Even science can't explain the randomness of magic

So remember good host about DNA
And the magickal world we can't truly explain

Imagination

Imagination is limitless, yes it is true
Imagination is only limited by you

You can inspire and gain some wonderful insight
From a wonderful hero fighting the good fight

A dragon so large, a giant so tall
Your mind can enhance the wonders of all

A destiny so noble or fated for a fight,
Your wyrd is your own, best have courage and might

Life can be hard or so it may seem
Remember every great story started as a dream

The imagination is the plan to have an idea
It can create great wonders but inspire your fear

Something so limitless and hard to restrain
The magic of hope and the magic of pain

Creation

Now comes the hard part in all that you do
Create a plan to make your dreams come true

Seidr is key and wisdom will grow
Plan for obstacles and defeat any foe

No path is without failure that truth is pure
You're tougher than you think there's a lot you can endure

When you feel low and your world is all pain
Remember every great journey has to go through the same

You don't need anyone to be your biggest fan
All you need is an idea followed by a great plan

Imagination and creation work together to seal
To turn a fantasy into something that is real

Although our futures are very unclear
Be brave and think and act without fear

So look through the fog and through the mist
Create your own world, do more than exist

Kinship

Listen here and listen close
Kinship is a magic that'll benefit you most

More than friendship, protect them as part of your kingdom
They help you grow within yourself with honour and wisdom

Kinship is not based on money or praise
But honour, respect and wisdom till the end of your days

Mutual gifting and sharing will be of great aid
With a good kin, a great life can be made

Selfless and lack of judgement are what keeps it true
With glory in mind, you only require a few

Kinship makes you feel much less alone
Keeps your oaths and promises like they're contracted in stone

Honour and glory to share with your clan
Never forget those that helped you develop your plan

Innergard you respect in all that you do
If the kinship is good they'll look after you too

Aspiration

Now you've had an idea and made a plan to follow through
Aspiration is what drives you to do what you do

For every dream, you hope for and desire
Your spirit inside burns hotter than fire

The more that you chase the life that you pursue
Your aspiration will earn what you are due

So whatever you do, do it with pride
Nothing burns hotter than the fire inside

The spirit you have develops your might
It's the difference between the size of the dog and the size of the fight

People's stories have surpassed more than others would have thought
It was the passion and desire behind each and every plot

So when you have an idea and a plan to follow
Make sure you aspire to manifest your tomorrow

Love

Now comes the magic to find it we fall
The reason we do what we do, the point of it all

We cannot describe, we cannot explain
It is the reason for joy but causes most of your pain

It can be a person, a pet or a thing that you do
No one can tell you what love means to you

Trying to define using logic that it defies
Beauty is judged in love's treasures, those beautiful eyes

Love is a treasure no money can buy
To find it you need more than one all-seeing eye

It can come anytime, a total surprise
A truth that is hidden right in front of your eyes

Love is so precious when you have it to hold
It grows into wisdom if you're smart when you're old

Love is a battlefield, with armour you'll fail
Only with trust, honour and mutual respect can love truly prevail

In the only fight, you hold a sword at the other's heart
One slip of the blade will leave you back at the start

Love is magic that nothing can define
Love is perceptual so keep that in mind

Wisdom

Wisdom is wandering and wondering just to explore
Wisdom is knowing there will always be more

Wisdom is insight, learning and discovering about you
Wisdom is uncovering a mystery while remaining true

Wisdom is starting a journey taking you far and wide
It will come with highs and lows just like the tide

Wisdom is knowing death might be near
Wisdom is acting despite the pressures and the fear

Wisdom is observing using more than your eyes
Wisdom is seeing the truth by deciphering the hows and the whys

Wisdom is memories filled with joys and sorrows
Wisdom is the memory you leave when you have no more tomorrows

That's why the world remains a magickal place, good host. An acronym from runes and poetry that's true. Life may be hard, and the earth is weary, but you must first regain your footing on mother earth. Stand fast and always be ready, for if you do not love yourself first how will you ever understand how to love another? The hope of the world exists in the children. Songs of hope, love and joy will aid them to break free from structure and become inspired.

My aim now is to seek out my widow and charm her heart once more. Despite her secluded and cold demeanour, her heart could still beat for our love once more. This world is cold now but knowledge without the power of love cannot triumph over the deception of intelligence. Loki will fall, I swore it once on Gungnir and I tell you now as a man. For if a man cannot keep his word, then he loses his honour and the respect of others.

Cailleach (Auld Lang Syne)

Should all acquaintances be forgotten and never brought to mind? No, but all acquaintances I have had over my lifetimes should be forgiven for times long past. My mortal lives required blood heirs so that I could continue generationally through the years. Sure I may have skipped a generation or three but I was there. I remained hidden through the ages only to plan and execute whatever I could while being limited to my short lifespans.

Flash forward a few thousand more lifetimes, when I fathered and mothered more children than I care to count. Although through the years I've always encouraged my children to believe in something other than Christianity. I have told them tales of gods and heroes, of monsters and men, of elves and fae, and dwarves and goblins. Each tale created a wondrous world more than the one that exists, but it was finally time to find mother earth. If we, as a people, or as gods, had any hope for the future, the old ways would have to return.

Through my travels, which took me from Russia to Africa and everywhere in between, there were whispers of a witch wherever I went. She'd be connected to earth magic and would only appear during the colder months. Some would say she was an old crone. Others called her a monster, but the truth is rarely so one-dimensional. I travelled lands where she was known as one of the fates, I wandered through parts of Midgard where she was known as Baba Yaga. I searched for signs of her in Sweden when she went by Gefjun and found tales of her as Frau Holle in Germany.

Wherever I wandered she always was forever ahead of me. It was such a turnaround when she used to follow me so. It wasn't until one day I visited the isle of Skye. I went there to mourn my son's passing but to also remind myself of my oath to him. He would be king again. I am not one to break my oath, not that I could, as I swore it on Gungnir.

While at the Storr collecting my thoughts and continuing my journey, I found a crack in the rocks. The sunlight glistened off something metallic, something glorious. I stuck my head in the dark space to look closer. It seemed to be a weapon of sorts, but I couldn't make out what type it was. Reaching into the space, I began prying it from rock and stone. Slowly, it revealed something familiar to me. It was Gungnir, the very spear I used in a time long past. After releasing it from its prison my mind raced with every oath made upon it. My mind seemed to guide me on where to go next.

Twilight of the Gods: Book of Skuld

I wandered to the centre of a town now established on Skye and I could hear the people whispering rumours. In local bars, in grocery shops, and even on the streets in casual conversation. Tales of lady hiding amongst the glens of Scotland. Secluded, she was happy and if anyone crossed her path, lightning would illuminate the skies and the earth would shake. People spoke in riddles suggesting no one survived an encounter but the people were wrong. If no one survived, then I wonder where the tales came from.

I began losing respect for the people from that place. They began calling her an old hag, a hideous witch and, in general, lost respect for mother earth. They were such fools. She had created the very lands they walked upon. She had shaped the beautiful landscapes with Mjolnir. She was the personification of the earth, and mother nature and the lands are a tribute to her beauty and splendour. The hammer she wielded belonged to another and it would be my duty to return it.

I don't even recall the name I went under at the time but while I called Scotland my home, I'd attempt to charm her. I travelled over the mounds and through the Glens, through cities and villages until whispers and rumours became a little more coherent. The men and women folk warned me of the danger but I had to warm my beloved's heart and return the hammer to my son. My Frigg mourned and wept alone but sometimes love is the warmth my lady needed.

Love is undefinable and people find it in all sorts of places in life. Some find it in work, and others find it in their children. Some find it through friendships, and others find it in special places. Myself, I see it in my beloved's eyes and enjoy walking her lands cautiously. I love the challenge that loving another brings. It makes you think of more than yourself, it allows you to grow and adapt. Knowing that I can say I love her at any given time or place makes my heart smile though I rarely show it on my face. I have eased her burdens with war. I honoured her love and protection of children when I was Santa. Now comes the challenge of reminding her of my vows and allowing her to see me again despite my outward appearance changing so much.

I approached a damp and dreary cave in Scotland after the rumours had led me there. It was not unlike the time I tried to make peace with Verdandi. The walls were covered in cobwebs, and I could hear her soft voice through the darkness. I carried a lantern in one hand and Gungnir in the other, using it as a staff to steady my feet. As I carefully trod deeper into the cave, her voice became agitated, and she began threatening me as I approached. Her voice was filled with so much anger and hatred toward the human race, but my heart fluttered the closer I got.

When your love is distant and cold, good host, approach with caution. Do not allow distance and silence to feed the wolf inside of her. It will be hard but sometimes being there to take the brunt of the hatred can stop the monster inside from growing exponentially. Be cautious with the words of your voice too because although they are spoken with reason, matters of the heart are seldom so straightforward.

Suddenly, a gust of wind extinguished the candle I carried. The cave was illuminated with a light blue glow. It felt magical and terrifying, but even I was amazed as hope returned to my head. She emerged from the shadows, both beautiful and powerful as I recalled. Her green eyes like the grassy meadows had turned blue as the sapphire on Brisingaman. Gnoss and Gersemi still sparkled beautifully in the blue light. Her red hair fell down her back like autumn leaves now burned brighter like her fiery temper.

"What do you want," asked the beautiful voice, as it boomed throughout the cave.

"Simply to gaze on your beauty and remind you of a few things, my Frigg."

"I haven't heard that name for an age. What makes you think I'd allow a stranger to call me such."

"I may look like a stranger, but you are only observing the surface. Would you prefer Freya?"

"I have gone by that name but only to one and he died a long time ago. You are bold to call me by these names, but I am not your beloved and I am not your lady."

"Apologies for overstepping but what can you tell me of him, the one long gone? Perhaps the memory might rekindle your thoughts and return the smile to your face."

"He was clever and charming. He knew exactly what to say and when to simply listen. He was my hero and a great leader. He fathered many of our children and he helped them grow into the ones they are now."

"Children? Where are they now? Can you tell me of them too?"

"Baldur was my innocent child. Wherever he was the world seemed happier and brighter. Unfortunately, he died long ago, and the world has grown colder because of it. People have become harsh towards one another and even the youth have lost their beliefs in the magickal world we live in."

"That is terrible, good lady. My heart aches for your loss. Are there any other children that may warm your heart?"

"Our firstborn, Ullr was as big as a bear. He fights for just causes. He even fought his father and won the right to lead, for a time. It was only his allegiance to that horrible wolf that made him give his right and his right hand to rule. He goes by Tyr now, but he has always made me proud."

"Sounds like a nobleman. Are there any others?"

"There are many I am proud to call my children, but one is the reason for my cold bitterness toward the world."

"Your child caused you so much grief to twist your heart? What did he do to cause your pain, Jörd?"

"You know my name, strange wanderer? Most call me by my title but few know my name. Mother Nature, Mother Earth, Frigg, Freya but fewer and fewer know my true name."

"My lips speak the words my heart knows. My mind sees you as you once were. And I swore a long time ago that I'd love you in this life and the next, until Ragnarök comes."

"You can't be him. He died and he never came back to me. You are a mortal but there is something familiar about the words of your voice. That spear though does look familiar."

"Look with your heart, not your eyes. If you can see beneath the surface, my love, you will know the truth. I am a god of death in mortal form. I am a giver of inspiration to every mortal that lives. I gift the children of the world with a reason to hold on, a reason to hope and a reason for the honour. I do this with a ho ho ho!"

"Odin it is you! Where have you been and who sits on the sky throne?"

"Loki killed my godly form with my spear. After he cursed my spirit into the monstrous Kraken. However, I had already sent Thor to release me from this cursed form. It was this very spear that saved me so long ago. My final oath to my blood brother, Loki, kept me from fading from existence. I have been everything over the years; man, woman and child. I have had children and written biblical tales simply to keep us alive deep in the minds and hearts of the human race."

"Why did you not come sooner? Why did you make me wait?"

"Loki sent his executioners for me. The Romans burned the pagans and slew them all. Then I came back as another, and he erased my testament in the bible. I kept coming back and he vilified me, executed me, and humiliated me. I had to bide my time and wait until the path was clear."

"What do you want from me now, my love?"

"I need that hammer. Thor killed me but it was I that sent him to purpose. I became the embodiment of a monstrous creature. I didn't have a hope in Helheim to gain my throne back as that. I need Thor to regain his purpose so we all can return to Asgard and reclaim our rightful place in the world."

"He shattered my heart long ago. I can't bear to face him now."

"You are stronger than you think, my love. The past is not to be judged it is simply a tool to learn. If you avoid or forget it how can we grow better? Action in the present will always be the best judgement of character. Go to him now and return his hammer."

"Here is your sack. This is the one that once contained Andalfari's treasure so long ago. It holds the hammer in it now. Take it to my son, with my deepest apologies. I will mend our broken bonds of family over a meal and drink at Aegir's hall. I wished I knew it was your plan all along."

Suddenly, loud haunting howls echoed throughout the dark night outside the cave. I grasped my spear knowing what monstrous puppets hunted me. They were the brave and noble werewolves of Valhöll but were now reduced to puppets for the self-proclaimed god in the heavens.

"There are no wolves in Scotland," Frigg curiously said.

"No, God has sent the Einherjar for me. I don't know if I'll survive this with this mortal form I possess now."

"Well, you have given my heart reason to flutter once more. So perhaps I have a gift for you, Odin."

The pool inside the dark cave began to ripple. I was face to face with a fiery horse creature with dead eyes. As it pranced forward, Sleipnir emerged behind it. Slowly, it approached staring into my very soul. I wasn't who I was before leaving me vulnerable to Hödr and Loki's attempt on my life. I stood unafraid holding my spear in one hand and my other outstretched toward the Kelpie. It rested its snout on my open palm knowing that deep beneath the mortal shell I wore was the god it once knew.

"Go now, find Thor, and let times long past be forgiven. I'll hold them off as long as I can. I'll find you again, Odin. My heart knows where to go."

I escaped to the back, as she turned to face the werewolves that hunted me. Jord fought bravely and her power was a lot more than a few werewolves could handle. Rock and stones, cut flesh and broke their bones. They quickly retreated knowing they were not a match for my beloved.

I galloped over the water, in the skies and the lands until I found the remnants of my boy. Tales of extraordinary strength and powerful battles with monstrous foes. He existed secretly in Midgard amongst the mortals but adopted the quiet life of a farmer. Still, sometimes the rumours of mortals held some fragments of truth. A mighty hero can only lie and deceive a little. It goes against their character and their values. They can't stand back and allow chaos to have power.

I would mend the bridge that was wrongfully burned long ago through my trickery and not sharing my plan. However, good host, if I had told my lady the plan, she may have revealed it to my enemy. The mortals would only appreciate me after I was gone. The gods had to be absent, so that darkness could prevail. It is only in our darkest moments that we truly gain wisdom from the light.

When our innocence dies, we must try to find it in others and keep it burning bright for as long as we are able. For the world is magickal and we must remember that as we hold onto hope with honour. Life is complex and understanding that many different world views exist is the wisdom of perspective. Each being has a different view of the world than you. Not wrong, simply different and that is the beauty of nature.

A Dark Winter's Night

I escaped the hunt of the Einherjar, and I knew my beloved still lived as the future still exists. She was the most powerful of goddesses I have ever known, and she had even bettered me in times long past. A pack of werewolves stood no hope for success against her magic and power over earth. Still, I moved across the skies with haste sliding through the clouds like snow as the day faded to darkness. I had to find the one I had resurrected from death so long ago. He could give me a gift that would make me stronger, faster and more articulate with my words. The Runes may have given me the ability to read people, gods or Jotuns but to speak in a way to deliver my intent, can rally the army needed to reclaim Asgard from Loki's control.

It takes time to grow and choose from which angle you wish to attack life, good host. Remain quiet through your growth and humble in your accomplishments. Victories do not determine the greatness of a person as many champions know. It takes many failures on the road to glory. Many successful people should be wise enough to realise that failure is always lurking, waiting for its moment. However, failures have brought much more wisdom than successes ever have.

During my youth, I studied magic, science, and religious myths, in secret, but lived my life under various job titles. Beyond the superficial surface of life, one phrase helped me live through the hardships of starting over again and again and again. Hold on to hope with honour. Of course, I abbreviated it to Ho Ho Ho because if you choose to do something, it should make you happy while you do it. That is after all the key to life.

In one of my many lifetimes, I read a book on Necromancy and discovered the science but also the mystery behind it. A large bolt of electricity from Thor's hammer resurrected his goats. I used the same magic on someone that some would call my monster. Only gods and Nornir are supposed to have powers over life and death but there is a way to bring people to life for a few moments at least. Enough to spark curiosity and joy in some, and dreadful fear in others. Once I tell you, remember it. It will give you comfort when those have left you and can never return.

Stories containing memories will take you to a time and a place in your mind. It will make you smile for but a moment. If you know of someone's uncomfortable past the very thought of someone's name brings dread and unease. I advise you to use it against your enemies. Manipulate their reaction to the desired outcome needed for you to succeed. I had to do this on an enemy of my past. A twisted creature, whose power I had to acquire to claim Hlidskjalf back.

This creature was one of the children my lady and I created while making peace with Vanaheim. His rebirth caused me to trick and manipulate another into loving me, while appearing as Baldur with Njord's feet. His killers were responsible for creating the very spear I wield now, but I required more from them. They had the same magic Loki took from Verdandi. One died by Perseus's hand and the other remained under the guise of an innkeeper.

I roamed the earth in search of the last of the dark elves. I searched every dark forest at the edge of every mountain. It was made more difficult without my throne that allowed me to see all and know more. First, I had to look for Bragi, the one I created long ago. He used to be mortal as Kvasir, but I had to use some dark magic when the Strigoi took him from me. He was the wisest of men and embodied everything I wished to be. He was wise yet caring. He shared his wisdom with people throughout Midgard. However, after he was resurrected, he became a recluse, withdrawn from the world. He hid in the shadows and hibernated through the ages.

Giving up my search for Eitri, I steered Sleipnir to Transylvania. I spoke with the people there and enjoyed their scary tales. Tales of a shadowy figure that feasted on blood and flesh. This creature managed to charm the hearts of women with the use of subtle sultry words. The wisdom of poetry is knowing what to speak and how to deliver it in a way that emotionally connects to the listeners. You see it even now, good host. Inspirational quotes, song lyrics and poetic metaphors. This would be a pearl of wisdom I would require while rallying an army to take on Heaven.

This creature of the night would have to be provoked out of hiding and convinced to join my quest. Lucky for me he liked to toy with his food and enjoyed quizzing his prey. He wished to treat his victims how he was treated when he became a victim himself. His strength was far beyond that of a Jotun, and he moved like a gust of wind. So, I could not battle such a foe. You could sense that he was around, but you could not see him unless he chose to reveal himself. That is why he must be provoked into a battle of the mind.

Many different languages called him many names from Nosferatu to count Dracula, but I knew his true name. I held onto hope that it would be enough to gain his aid in locating Verdandi's magically enchanted dark elf. I would have to remain tactful and keep my wits about me when approaching and provoking this former friend. I couldn't walk as Odin but instead used the name, Sinterklaas.

Twilight of the Gods: Book of Skuld

After I gathered as much information from the surrounding villages as I could, I prepared for my encounter. I searched my magical sack and found the freshest apples. They were Idunn's, a lucky find for his mind may be bitter but his love remained. They gave the gift of youth and health to the gods when they feasted on them so long ago.

Sometimes a weapon does not need to be made of steel or wood, good host. An attack of the heart through the mind can weaken even the strongest of foes. Idunn had left him long ago but perhaps an oath for their reunion may be the drive he needs to join my quest. Solitude is good for a while, there can be strength found there. A strength of knowing you can stand alone. However, for one's world to grow the adaptability one must acquire for love to work. In all my years of wandering love requires three things: trust, mutual respect and lastly support. Support a common goal whether you must invest from afar or cheer in the audience.

I knew Bragi would no longer recognise me as a man but perhaps my wit can spark some familiarity in his mind. After all, I still had some residual memory of the mead of poetry in my soul. If I could get another draught, then I would regain a power that would aid me in the fight against Loki.

I made my approach to his castle at night. Being nocturnal, it would have been rude to interrupt his sleep. The clouds blanketed the sky, extinguishing any light that appeared in the area. The stories of priests dying in their attempts to exorcise a demon, haunted my thoughts. They were ill-prepared. They came thinking if they invoked the power of God, they would have destroyed this vampire. Sadly, they found the truth in their final moments.

With each step, I could feel my heart pound a little harder. The stench of rotten corpses became more overwhelming the closer I got to the entrance. The wood appeared rotten, and the castle looked like it had fallen into ruin. I had a gut feeling I was being watched but it didn't matter, I had to proceed. I had to gain knowledge and remind him of what was lost.

I approached the door with my sack over my shoulder. It was a large door, not as large as the ones in Jotunheim but still large enough to haunt my soul. The breeze vanished and the air became deathly still. There were no signs of life here, no sounds of animals, just darkness and death. Heads impaled on spikes with their haunting expressions would have turned most heroes into frightened children, but I pressed on.

With every ounce of strength, I could muster, I pushed the doors open. Suddenly, a colony of bats rushed me. Their screeches echoed through the darkness as their fluttering wings deafened me momentarily. I dropped my sack and an apple rolled out as the bats dispersed. I quickly gathered it, knowing I was being stalked by a predator unlike any other. I walked to the centre of the hall, in front of an enormous staircase leading me further into the darkness. Scanning my surroundings, I found more signs of death with warnings written in blood.

Those bloodstained walls told me to run and get out while I still could. In some places, I found decayed bones of heroes that had fallen. The internal structure seemed weary with the years that they had endured. The wooden staircase showed signs of decay and cobwebs were in almost every corner. I approached each of the remains to study them further. I figured if I could identify at least one of the fallen, I could verify the myths I was told.

"Get out now!" A haunting voice roared from the shadows. "Leave before I take your life!"

"I will not! I am merely an old wanderer, seeking hospitality. Is this how you treat your guests, old one?"

"You are nothing more than a fly, old man. A fly on my web that I am about to drink. Tell me what is stopping me from draining you dry?"

"Curiosity and you would be a fool to think of me as a fly in this encounter. I could have come with a sword or pitchfork and flame but instead, I came with a gift to remind you of your name."

"Flame and name… rhyming poetry? And a gift? I hate to say the third is impossible. None alive remember my name and it exists as a foggy memory within me. You are a professor of sorts are you not? What is your name?"

"I am Professor Abraham Van Helsing and I have studied much. What I have discovered may help clear the fog in your mind, ho ho ho. Tell me what you think your name is."

"Very well I'll play your game Van Helsing but if I guess it then your life will be forfeited."

"Sure, you can get a guess for every gift I give you, here's your first. If you do not guess your name, then you must gift me with something in return. You must grant me immortality," I said revealing nine juicy yellow apples from my sack.

"Very well, this won't take long. My name is Dracula," the vampire said while crunching on the apple.

"Wrong," I said as he devoured the apple in haste.

"Prince of Darkness," he said devouring the next apple.

"Wrong again, friend. That is a title"

"Antichrist!"

"Wrong again."

This continued back and forward and with every apple came another incorrect guess. It will always be a sad thing if you forget yourself due to the minds of lesser folk. People may say things nasty about you and call you some version of a monster, but it only becomes true if you forget yourself.

"Tell me, do you know why I brought apples? Have you ever read one of the Bibles of these now-deceased priests? Do you know of Adam and the myth of the apple?"

It came to the final guess and the vampire searched his mind for his name. He strained and paced as he tried to gather himself to give his final answer. He devoured the final apple and wiped his face from any residue.

"My name is Askr, the original untwisted tale of Adam!"

"Wrong! None should brag about being the father of humans. I know, I don't."

"You choose your words oddly, old man."

"I choose my words wisely, vampire. The first clue I gave you was the challenge in poetic rhyme. The second clue was the golden apples I gifted you to remind you of the one you loved. The third clue was Adam and apple myth to remind you of your love. The name of the garden, good host. Your lover, Idunn. Every word I shared was a clue to who you are. You are Bragi the god of poetry, lover of Idunn and formerly known as the wise Kvasir. You are the living contract of peace between the Vanir and Aesir and you can bring us together again."

"Where is my Idunn if you speak the truth?"

"She has been cursed as an angel but if you give me immortality, I swear to reunite you. I will take the heavens back for the gods of Asgard."

"Take my blood, old man. I will aid you with what you need. I still can't work out if we've met before wanderer."

"After I return with the immortal gift, I shall reveal my true identity."

Bragi bit down on his wrist, drawing blood. He held his wrist to my mouth as I drank deeply. The power was intoxicating. I could feel the power surging through my veins. My skin turned cold but became as tough as ice itself. I took just what I needed. I gained the power of Gilling and his wife, along with Kvasir's wisdom. I now had the tools needed to get my family together again.

I helped Bragi up to his feet and in the blink of an eye, I left and returned with a deer. He sank his fangs into its neck restoring his strength by draining it dry. Suddenly, wolves howled in the distance. The Einherjar were closing in on us. This time I couldn't die, so we fought together. We slew the three that hunted us sending them back to my hall.

Under the cover of darkness, we retreated. There was much more to do. I had to claim Verdandi's magic to beat Loki. I had to reunite the gods, I had to raise an army of Jotuns, and I had to reclaim what was taken through trickery and deception.

Sinterklaas

Kvasir and I slid through dark forests, sticking to the shadows during the daylight. Although we could move quickly, I still used Sleipnir to get around. The lands were so merged it was difficult to differentiate between them. We were hunting for the living remanence of Verdandi's magic. With my heightened senses, I could smell it in the air. Only one being remained alive over the millennia. The Jotuns were burned and killed mercilessly by Loki's followers to the point of almost extinction.

Most retreated to the more desolate places of the world. They remained as nothing more than superstitious stories. Tales that explained the missing people, the travellers that had succumbed to death. If remains were found the wildlife would be to blame. Some were never seen or heard from ever again, even the bones were consumed or repurposed as tools for the surviving Jotuns. A mighty race now reduced to some sort of demonic ghost story made me weep.

We avoided any encounter with the living because we couldn't afford to slow our pace. The distance was far and the journey hard, but I was more driven to accomplish this task and uphold my oaths. It was the only path I could take to defeat Loki. When we neared villages, we would stop to hear their tales and gather more information on our target. The thirst for blood was difficult to subdue but my mind was stronger than my body's desires.

Tales of glowing yellow eyes and a dark forest creature started to make most run from their mere mention. The creature moved quickly and as silent as a breeze. It was shorter than a man, not much taller than a child. It stalked its prey for three nights before draining them of their blood. Some said it was a bat-like goblin and others said it was a child with death following close by. Whenever we asked, it gave the locals an uneasy feeling to speak of such a creature. They did not wish to provoke it to hunt them.

Suddenly, a woman's scream came from the darkness of the forest. Blood-curdling screams that were like nails on a chalkboard. It was too faint for the human ear to detect but it sounded like it was only a few feet away from me. You could feel the terror and the anguish in your soul. I rose from my place by the fire and disappeared in an instant. I ran faster than I have ever run before. It was like time stood still as I moved through the land. I could see and hear the animals move slowly as my feet pounded the ground. Even the wind appeared to pause as I was swift to purpose.

Reaching the source of the screams, I was too late. I settled her like a father would a child waking from a night terror. Easing her panic as her heartbeat slowed. The woman lifted her head from my chest to meet my eyes. I kept my fangs concealed to reduce the fear in the woman. I was only but a moment too late, but I hated failure. Her eyes became cold and lifeless as the colour of her face drained away.

"What has happened little one?"

"I... I have seen it."

"What did you see little one?"

"Eyes glowing yellow, it moved amongst the trees. It was terrible," the lady wept in fright.

"Which direction?"

"It was westward. I could see a building in the distance. The building was too big for a home and was too little to be a castle."

I looked at Kvasir concealed by the forest as if I was telepathically telling him, "let's go." The lady died shortly after and I left the body in the fire. I did not wish the mortals to become prey to any more vampiric creatures. We moved as humans swiftly towards the tree line. After we were embraced by the cover of darkness, we moved much more quickly. My purpose was to gain Verdandi's magic only to challenge Loki. A challenging quest that required two more to resurrect from Helheim first.

Finally, we located the building. It was the darkest time of night. The trees moaned as even the gentlest of breezes made them bend to its will. No animal could be found for miles, they feared this place. It smelt and felt like death awaited beyond the entry. The lights were on but only the clinking of glasses could be heard as we kept our distance. My eyes focused on the sign that hung above the doorway. It had been worn with time but with my enhanced senses, I could decipher what it once said. "Fjalar's inn."

As the plan developed in my head, I instructed Kvasir on what to do. First, I'd have to ensure we were alone. No Jotun or dark elf other than Fjalar could be in the bar. Thanks to the magic I received from the mead of poetry from Kvasir's veins, I knew the words that would deliver the outcome I required. I also knew how to deliver them in such a way that would incite fear and panic among the Jotuns and Dark elves.

I bit down on my wrist and filled two separate bottles with my blood. I gave them to Kvasir and instructed him on what to do. I knew two corpses still existed in the basement from the past, like trophies. It weakened me almost to the point of death, but it was necessary. Fjalar's death would come from the hands of those that he had killed. Urd had a way of always catching up to you. Even though she was gone her ways were still strong.

I stumbled through trees until I made it to the door. With my last ounce of strength, I pushed through the door and dragged myself into a chair. I used Gungnir to steady myself and deliver a warning to all who were inside. If they did not leave, God's judgement will be swift and smite all those that stayed. It felt awkward saying it, and Fjalar knew. However, the customers at his bar did not hang around to test my resolve.

The power of Christianity had struck fear in those that once forced humanity to cower and run in terror. A religion that is more monstrous that even land spirits and monsters of great power now hide from.

"Well, now that you have sent my customers running, I may inquire as to what it is that you want, old man. You barely have much life to cling to. I can hear your heartbeat slow, although it still beats deep like a war drum," the barkeep mocked.

"I require a drink to regain my strength. You are fond of a drink or three or so the rumours go."

"Careful, old man. The words of your voice seem to carry the stench of accusation on them. I could snuff you like a wick."

"You would not demean your greatness by killing a weak old man, would you? I am simply looking to pass time before my guests arrive."

"You are expecting company?"

"Yes, and you know them well."

"Perhaps you can refresh my memory."

"Let me think... You reduced one of my guests to tears when you broke her heart."

"I have had many lovers, and all were sad when I sent them away."

"She did not love you. My second guest was a king. His son visited you a long time ago after the king had drowned in sorrow."

"Many come and claim royalty. Many more have drowned their sorrows; it is a bar after all. Children are the easiest of prey."

"You are as slippery as a serpent Eitri, but not all serpents can swim, can they?"

"Eitri? I haven't heard that name in a while. I am not a snake old man."

"Not all snakes slither in this day and age. Most use power, lies and treachery to bite you when you are unaware. Would you prefer Fjalar?"

"You know my name, but I am unaware of yours, old man. Care to enlighten me?"

"My name is Sinterklaas, and I know what you have done, little dark elf. You no longer have your brother's company and I need something from you."

"I will give you nothing but a swift death!"

"But I haven't spoken of my third guest. He was wise and had a heart purer than my own. He wandered as I did long ago, but he only wished to share knowledge and wisdom. You took advantage of his young heart and made him suffer."

Suddenly, the cellar door burst open and three rose from the deep dark depths. Fjalar fell back in shock, startled by the sight of the three undead faces that I previously described. He stumbled back unable to catch a breath. He was frozen in terror as Kvasir, Gilling and his wife moved toward him. Each step they took toward the Strigoi sent him scrambling backward. Before Fjalar got to the door Kvasir was waiting with fangs drawn. Gilling and his wife held him in place while I walked toward him from my stool. He twisted and struggled but his strength couldn't compare.

Smiling in front of his face, I revealed my fangs. I sank them into his jugular vein with haste. I drank deeply, draining him to a skeleton, with only skin draped from his bones. With a surge of power flowing through my veins, I felt more powerful than before. I had gained Verdandi's magic, and my strength was far greater than what I had before. I had not only gained power in the physical sense but now I was able to use magic far beyond anything I could use as a mortal or a god.

As he lay there drained of his blood, I reached down collecting something that caught my eye. It was his red hat stained with the blood of those too foolish or trusting enough to cross the threshold without being aware of enemies. It stood out in contrast of the white snow that fell from the skies. Perhaps it was once a symbol for death but now I'd repurpose it as a symbol of hope. A magic red hat, that snow only seemed to settle at its point and brim. Through the darkest of nights and the coldest of times, I will hold onto hope with honour until glory is mine.

From that moment on, I was faster than Kvasir and stronger than Thor. I had abilities of magical proportion, like my Freya taught me so long ago. Now I had the power to defeat Loki, the only trouble was, I couldn't do it alone. The power of kinship Loki had removed from the word magickal proved to hint towards his weakness.

I looked toward Iceland for tales of monsters, witches, Yule lads and Yule cats. I sought to reunite with an old flame that gave refuge to my kin. Her name had evolved to Gryla but back in the days of old, it was Gríðr. A powerful Jotun witch that gifted Thor his belt and gauntlets, and she gifted me a son that would avenge my death and guide others in the next life.

Yule Cats

From deep in the heart of the forests in Europe, I travelled to Iceland. It was December, and the cold had her grasp on the land. Everyone sought shelter in their homes, simply trying to survive the cold and the darkness. The people became fearful of unwelcome guests and all kinds of creatures during this year. They'd burn the Yule log for three days and nights to survive the Krampus or Gríðr or even the irritation of the Yule lads.

As I wandered alone, I peeked through cracks in blinds and holes in doors. Loki had vilified and transformed all matters of creatures in these lands. He had turned the Yule season into a time of fear and survival. Clever Loki, trying to reduce any aid given to me by the people. I'd have to rely on storytelling and gift-giving to sway their minds. Fear can be a weapon for control but can inspire the brave to rise. The bold continue to survive because knowledge is power.

I knocked on the first door I came across and received no answer. I couldn't enter a home without being invited by the owner. No guest should ever enter without a proper invitation. Being an unexpected visitor was inappropriate enough, without imposing myself on them. It's an old myth that has been tied to vampires but, it is the teachings of the Hávamál.

I did not require the blood of the innocent to sustain myself anymore. The power of Verdandi I had gained elevated me above that. I walked through time existing as it came to be. My presence was my present to those that needed something more. I was an idol that protects and gives hope and joy in the dark and cold times of the year. I came during the night, so that the dawn of the next day brought joy from the darkness, hope from despair and most of all knitted the kin together through the festive season.

After two failed attempts to gain entry, I left coal on their doorstep. It wasn't as a punishment, just a gift to keep their homes warm in Yule. After, I approached more of a shack than a house. Then again, it didn't have to be much, it only had to provide comforting shelter. A home is far better than an empty mansion or a house full of false friends. The family there was not as well off as others and required warmth for survival. The children were cold and sick. Their lives would have ended if not for my intervention. I knocked on the door and they opened it quickly eager for aid and company by the fireplace.

They began speaking of the terrible tales which taught their children the value of behaving and being helpful to the household, in the approach of the winter solstice. The life of a child, although innocent, must not be free from aiding the household. The cold and harsh times bring the need for warmth and new clothing. I pulled the purest of black coal and tossed it in the fireplace. It burned hotter than any wood and gave a warm glow to the home. We continued to discuss as I pulled a feast from my sack. We ate, we told tales and we celebrated late into the night.

Suddenly, my heightened senses could hear an unusual sound outside. It was faint to most but to me, it was more like an engine idling. The ground shook but only strong enough that I could feel it. Whatever approached was large but light on its feet. Slowly, I developed a picture in my head. I could feel the steps, I could hear the noise and the smell was familiar to me. Two felines approached stealthily. Their steps were light in the snow as they stalked their prey. They were larger than normal cats, bigger than a bear. As they drew near the house, I knew they would take the children if I never acted.

Such majestic beasts but almost repurposed to destroy rather than aid the earth. Cats were gifted to newly married couples in ancient times to keep their homes free from pests. Cats used to be worshipped and respected as symbols of protection linked to a motherly goddess in most lands. They were my lady's, no, my beloved's cats cursed to take hope from those with very little. Loki was clever but vindictive. Any link to the light returning after winter solstice he'd extinguish. Any pagan traditions or practices, he would vilify.

I reached deep into the sack and pulled out new clothing for the entire family. Socks, jackets, jumpers that were freshly knitted. There was enough to keep them warm even if the coal burned no longer. The deafening purring faded as the cats no longer had their prey. Their earth-trembling steps vanished almost so faintly that even my senses could barely detect them. The family was most grateful, which brought me joy, but I had to leave. I had to find these creatures not only for myself but for another. They would be a gift to remind the future of the past.

As soon as I closed the door I ran swiftly toward the cats. Travelling so quickly, I never left a footprint in the snow. I followed their scent in the air. Suddenly, through the darkness and blizzards, I was confronted. It appeared to be the normal size of a cat, but it had a magical aura surrounding it. The cat hissed as it lowered its head and moved toward me, stalking its prey. With every step, it doubled in size. If I was still mortal, I would have been terrified. Staring deeply into its eyes I saw its soul. It had been abandoned, tortured and mistreated over the years by Loki's, followers. My heart ached as I could see all the cat had endured. I read the three scars that indicate the drive behind one's actions. The physical scars that appear on the surface, and the emotional trauma experienced over their history. The mental scars caused by the previous two traumas. I held the cat's gaze while my ears scanned for the other.

The cat was the size of a house towering over me. As it moved toward me, I lowered my hood. I winked toward the cat, as I stood tall and smiled in the face of danger. I was familiar with it, as if it searched my scent. I held my hand out to scratch its chin and it began to shrink. I read the cat's tag but it held only half a message. "This cat belongs to Freya," it read. I picked the cat up carefully and placed it gently into my sack, before I used my senses to track the other.

I approached the other with haste with my red cap upon my head. The snow pelted me as I floated through the darkness. Some of the snow collected and stuck to the peak of my hat. The next cat was approaching a house. The children within hadn't received new clothes for Yule. I jumped as high as I could and landed on the monstrous cat's back. I began to scratch at the base of its tail. Its monstrous look fell from its face as it began to return to its house cat size.

The cat smiled as it began rubbing its face against my leg. It was good fortune that the cat recognised me too. I bent down to scratch its chin and looked at the collar. It purred and closed its eyes in enjoyment. The snowfall became lighter as the threat of the Yule cats lowered. The tag on the collar read, "if found return to Gríðr at Víðgelmir." I turned the tag over and from the flat metallic plate appeared a map. It was a map of Iceland with the witch's location. I carefully placed the second cat in my sack, to return it to my beloved Jörd.

I headed west, over mountains, through towns and navigating the nature of forests. The sun no longer burned my skin. The power of Verdandi had made me far more powerful than any vampiric creature. I was faster than Huginn, inspired by Muninn and I rose to something more. I was a god of knowledge, wisdom, and death.

First, I was a warrior, and then I brokered peace between the realms. I rose to the throne as a leader of gods and fell to the limitations of a mortal. To defeat Lucifer and God I had to break free from the shackles of limitations of mortality. A man became a myth. A myth became a legend, and a legend becomes a god. I will claim Asgard and Hlidskjalf but I cannot do it alone.

My goal was to reinstall the Nornir to their influential role. Without respect for Urd, Verdandi will trick and torment, leaving Skuld looking bleak. Without knowledge from the past, the present is doomed to torture your future. Learn from the past, live in the present and look toward the future. Three consistent mistresses of fate. My generation may have lost them but perhaps I will gift them to the next.

Gríðr and the Yule Lads

I rode Sleipnir with Prancer to Víðgelmir with haste. Over the skies and the seas at great speed. The clouds felt like snow and the air was so thin. I lost myself in the peacefulness of it all, but my mind never forgot its promise. A promise made many lifetimes ago when the world was much simpler. It would be the one thing that drove me throughout my mortal lifetimes.

An oath can be powerful beyond any measure of courage or strength. If one honours it, and upholds it, even throughout the hard times it builds character. Even if others break the oath toward you and you continue to uphold your end, then honour is yours. It helps us rise above those poor of character and gain respect for ourselves. If those who are not wise enough to see the oath you upheld, despite the other side no,t then fools they will remain.

My sleigh sank beneath the thick clouds down towards the icy caves. I slapped Prancer's hind, sending him off toward the nearest body of inland water. The nature of the Kelpie was always to wallow in the murky depths of inland water. Yes, it provides danger to mortals but at this point, mortals have a few million more than they should. It reduced the number of the foolish in the land. Those unwise enough to succumb to bad luck and poor choice.

Slowly, I approached the large and imposing entrance. The calling of crows echoed on the breeze and carried a horrible chill. I could see only darkness within. I suppose when you are trying to challenge a god, especially a god of darkness. A god that is attempting to be the guiding light, a little darkness goes a long way.

Deeper I went until all the light faded from sight. The silence was deafening but I still wandered deeper. The smell of the dampness was overpowering. I blindly navigated, feeling my way through the cold and wet cave walls. It appeared I was alone, yet I could feel the presence of greatness all around me. I called out to gain some sort of response that the cave wasn't abandoned.

Suddenly, a haunting whispering and giggling could be heard within. A bright glow lit up the cave, guiding me to a large open space. My eyes took a while to adjust to the light but slowly a familiar face emerged. She had aged over the years, but she still had a beautifully strong presence. Her skin was pale like snow, and she appeared serious holding her staff.

"What do you want, weary old man?"

"You used to be more patient in your younger days, Gryla."

"The world is less patient now and I do not have much time left. If you knew me in my younger days what was my name?"

"Time is indeed the most valuable currency and spending it with patience has gifted me calmness in the chaos. I have had a long life and spent many of my lifetimes developing myself. We had a child once when you went by Gríðr. It was long ago but he was strong. He taught me strength in remaining quiet."

"I have had only one biological child, but I do care for more."

"Ah, your Yule lads. I sent you one to care for, he was a brother of mine."

"If you can remember his name, his original name, I will know who you are. If you are who you say you are, you will know all three of your brother's names. What was his name when I accepted to protect him?"

"His name when I sent him to you was Heimdall."

"Correct, one down two to go. What was his name when he visited the world of men?"

"When he visited the humans, he was known as Rig."

"Few are aware of this than most. He is a great warrior that shaped the world by slaying a titan. What was his first name?"

"Let me think, it has been more than a few ages since I called him by another name. He was my brother and he helped me shape the worlds of men and women. His name was Ve."

"Odin! It is you! Your appearance has changed a lot. I have some of your kin but not all. Vidar, Honir, Heimdall, Tyr, and Njord to name a few. Even your queen has asked for refuge from Loki's persistent quest for power and control."

"Thank you Gríðr, for everything you have done. I have gifts for you all. For Vidar, I have a Bonsai tree. May its maintenance bring you strength in your calm. For Honir a phrase that encapsulates life. Hold onto hope with honour. Ho ho ho. For Tyr, a word weaved into Loki and Hödr's followers, Hallelujah! A play on hail Ullr to celebrate the god of glory, bravery, and justice. For Njord, here is a trident may you wield it well in the fight to come. Heimdall, my brother, only you can bring your child to justice. He is very clever and extremely powerful. You defeated him once but here is a sword. If reasoning fails, then always be ready to use your Hed. And finally, my love. Here are your precious cats may they pull you into battle and ensure your victory over your enemies. May we all meet on the Rhode to glory. It is only in the depths of our waves of thought that we truly are challenged to find the path to take. I have two more to visit and gift."

"Brother, take this, it will beacon one to meet with you. A gold tooth from a god is too precious for him to send any other fairy to collect. Freyr will come and you can convince him to join our cause."

Heimdall reached deep into his mouth. His face squinted and after a struggle, he plucked it out. He spat blood on the floor, but the tooth gave light to our overwhelming situation. The cave and all the gods looked hopeful towards the dire situation we must face. We all looked in awe as we waited for Freyr to arrive.

Moments passed and the sound of trotters clopped over the stones outside the cave. A bright light shone from the entrance you would have thought it daylight. The sounds evolved from hooves to footsteps as whatever was outside approached. It was eerie as all the gods drew their weapons in preparation for a mighty battle.

Suddenly, a familiar face appeared from the shadows. "Look at all these gods. All huddled together in a cave. Witches, a bear and a seal but they are all too weak without the boar king."

"Pigs can fly, little lord," my voice boomed throughout the cave.

"Odin? I thought you were…well dead."

"Really? Then you know who sits on the throne?"

"Loki, his powers and influence in this world surpass even yours."

"Do you recall my gift to you long ago?"

"It has inspired me to keep the innocence alive since the death of Baldur."

"You would think you would hold a manlier title than fairy," Tyr interrupted.

"Silence bear, before I go berserk. Innocence can be protected and inspired with more than might. I admire and respect him for becoming the tooth fairy." Tyr huffed and returned to silence.

"What is the plan Allfather?" Freyr asked standing ready to join.

"You command a legion of Elves, fairies and nymphs. We need them to attack the pearly gates Loki installed. Drawing out the Valkyrie turned into angels. This will create a distraction that will allow us to enter Valhöll and claim it back. He has great power but so do we. Together we can make him answer for his crimes. Crimes against us, crimes against humans and even against the Jotun race he demonised. What say you?" I called loud and proud to have their word and answer for the plan to attack.

"Let us get aid from Aegir and Ran. With the aid of the Jotun, the elves and the dark elves. Asgard can be reclaimed with less bloodshed," my beloved lady Jörd suggested wisely.

"I shall meet you there. I must go to Norway and get Thor to help. He's the only one Loki is intimidated by. And with his hammer back he will be a force to silence Loki's forked tongue."

The cave burst into one unified voice and purpose. The gods of Asgard will rise and reclaim the sky realm. Hlidskjalf will return to the rightful ruler of the nine realms once more. It is always better to win a fight from a position of strength, but glory comes from the rising of those seen to be weaker than their adversaries.

Tomtenisse

Have you ever been called something you aren't? Has someone exaggerated something you have done to paint your image in a different way from the truth? I mean, I am not short by any means but in comparison to someone like Thor, even the tallest of heroes looks puny and weak.

My journey took me far from Iceland to the mountainous landscape surrounded by beautiful waters in Norway. It was still Yule time although the calenders had changed throughout the years. Some celebrated during the start of December, others waited until the winter solstice, and some followed the old ways during the first full moon in January. With Loki's eradication of Urd, specific dates and times were jumbled for the festive season, but it did not matter. As long as it brought kin together in feast and celebration of hard times past or surviving another year despite the foes we face or challenges we have overcome.

My investigations into the location of Thor lead me from farmhouse to barn. I'd stay a night, maintaining and caring for the animals. Horses were my favourite as I loved to pass the time braiding and plating their hair. Soon my occupation was rumoured throughout the lands in the North. A spirit that required a feast or a food offering in exchange for a good harvest or well-maintained farm animals.

Rumours around these lands caught my ear of a giant farmer with a wife with golden hair. They had three children: a large boy with a mighty physique, a boy with courage and bravery to help those in need of it and a younger daughter with the strength to pull both into line. My mind pieced together the ancient stories to gain a fresh perspective of the present. They couldn't remain in the same lands for too long for fear of being discovered. Every nine years the family would sell their lands and travel before beginning again.

On the first day, I occupied his barn and braided his horse's hair, just like I did the other farms on my journey. During the early hours of the second morning, before anyone woke, I harvested crops of spinach and broccoli to ease the burden of work for my son and his family. It was the least I could do while remaining hidden from sight. Brushing and maintaining the animals while cleaning the barn started to spark wonder in his children.

They were more capable than an army of workers with their godly abilities, but the mind begins to wonder when times become easier. Less work than they were accustomed, made them think of supernatural entities at play. A Jotun, an elf or something else. Thor didn't fear anyone or anything because he was strength personified. No foe he faced stood a chance; no enemy could stand toe to toe without succumbing to death. He was physically unbeatable but that was only with his hammer.

I remembered a time I taught him lessons in life. Lessons of true heroism with honour and character. I taught him that no matter how much ale you can consume, it does not make you more of a hero. It reduces the mind's ability to absorb information, analyse the situation and leave you thoughtless with nothing but a sore head the next day.

I thought of another lesson about not raising one's ego in love. It will leave you deeper in the depths of depression when the weight of your ego shakes your very foundations. Egotistic behaviour is toxic and venomous, with the words we say to belittle others and falsely elevate ourselves. Life will humble you if you are wise enough to learn from it.

I recalled a third lesson; it was one that only those that survive long enough will endure. When our physical strength and our skills and abilities fade from us. When old age sets in, leaving nothing but the adaptation for it. Fighting is for the strong and fit. The wise are left to teach and instruct those warriors in their youth because in the end, old age comes to us all and weakens us over time. Letting go of the past to gain power over the present is the hardest thing anyone must conquer.

On the third night, I approached the large imposing doors to his residence. They were twice as tall as any normal house door. They had a dark varnish over the grain of the solid oak they were fashioned from. They had large and thick handles with door knockers that were held in place by cast iron lions' mouths. A symbol of pride, just like a group of lions gather. I attempted to convince Thor and his family to the great gathering of the gods.

As the heavy doors opened, I was dwarfed by my son standing in front of me. He was a huge man that onlookers from a distance would have seen me as a little over half his height. With my red cap and my blue cloak over my shoulders, it would have been a simple mistake that people of that country would have viewed me as a dwarf.

"What do you want little man?" Thor's voice boomed.

"Greetings to you, I have arrived. Where shall I sit? Only a fool would rely on luck when being hosted by a stranger. Warmth and comfort are needed for legs that a numb. Food and clean clothes are necessary for those that have wandered far in mind and on land. Gracious host, allow me to make myself presentable. May we share courteous words and silence so I may tell my tale? I know a lot, including you. But knowledge does not determine the value of a person. Instead, I share only what is needed. That is the reason I will rarely make mistakes. Know that I do not talk much, but when I do, you had better listen. My name is unimportant; my role is not your concern. I am simply a weary old man that requires some hospitality in exchange for a grand tale to tell. Would you be so kind as to share your time with a tired old man?" I asked while placing my sack on the ground from over my shoulder.

Thor humphed as he nodded to allow me into his home. He guided me to where I could wash my hands and seated me by the fireplace on the cold winter night. A hearty meal was prepared by Sif and the kids gathered around as they weren't used to visitors. I brought them gifts and shared wisdom of ancient tales of their father from years long past. Their faces lit up as they were inspired by the heroism of their father, who now remains with his back turned to the humans, only helping them with food.

"There is something we need to discuss after the meal, good host," I said to my son.

He looked straight through me without any sign of reaction.

"I have a gift for you, from your mother," I said pulling my sack closer to me.

"My mother is dead to me. She turned her back on me and my family long ago," Thor grumbled.

I pulled from my sack an idol made of straw. It was a Jólbukk and as I waved my hand over it, casting a magic spell. Slowly, it began changing into the form of a real goat.

"Magic? Are you a Jotun?" Thor questioned as his fists clenched rising from his chair.

"Not entirely but I do need your magic to give Heiðrún life once more. I know of your mother's actions, good host, but she did not know of your father's will."

"I do not have something that my mother had taken from me. I cannot resurrect my father's goat. He was just as bad, he told me my mother was dead and stood by as my mother banished me."

"Not everything is what it appeared to be, good host. Another sat on the throne of Asgard, a shapeshifter. He told you your mother was dead to keep you from returning and aiding the gods in battle. He stood idly by as your mother's broken heart cast you out. Once I told her the truth behind your quest, she was covered in shame and regret."

"She took my weapon! She wouldn't even allow me to explain myself! It has been an age since I have seen her. She doesn't care for me or my kin," Thor sulked.

I reached into my sack pulling out the hammer he once wielded long ago. His face began to lift from the sight of it. The first time I had seen him crack what looked like a smile in three days. Even the children's eyes widened at the sight of it. Mjolnir wasn't the most perfectly crafted weapon but even with its flaws, it brought Thor's realisation of his self-worth.

He waved the hammer over the Jólbukk and Heiðrún rose from the dead. It still had a little mead left but it would have to be returned to Asgard to feed on the foliage of Læraðr to produce more. I filled our cups and toasted the host and his family for their generous accommodation. They hosted a weary wanderer while remaining honourable hosts. Sadly, an aspect that has faded over the years.

"Who are you, old man?"

"I have many names in many lands. I have many titles in my various roles but you, good host, may call me father."

"Odin? Is it you?"

"It is and I need you to meet me at Aegir's hall. There the gods will gather with the Jotuns and Vanir. There we will discuss our plans for battle and war. There we will claim back the Skylands from manipulating fingers and a god reliant on leading the blind. What say you, boy? Will you join us in our rise to godhood once more?"

"I say to pour the mead from the goat and let us drink to commemorate the gods rising once more! I swear by Mjolnir I will meet you at Aegir's palace under the water. Although it has been a while can you give me directions?"

"The Rhode to glory is paved with the blood of Ymir. The whale's road will take you deep but stand fast because only you can silence a venomous tongue."

I use riddles to keep the mind sharp like a sword before the battle. Wit must be developed by challenging one's mind to search for answers to puzzles yet to reveal themselves. To read the runes you must look deeper than the words being spoken and see the letters that have your fate written.

Scrooge (Lokasenna)

The journey was long, but Prancer pulled the sleigh through the skies above. Winter's chill had a grasp of the world, but my mind searched for plans and plots to convince the Vanir to join me once more. Through the cold crisp night, I travelled south, towards Greece. I needed to locate the entry to Vanaheim as the world had changed from the times of old and the lands had drifted from their original location.

There were three beautiful islands to choose from in the Aegean Sea; Santorini, Samos and Rhodes. My cryptic riddle had revealed which island to choose, I only hoped the rest of the gods had discovered its truth as I waited for them to arrive. I paced on the sand, while I thought deeply about my many different lives in the past.

First, I remembered when I was king of Troy, under the name of Priam. War desolated my kingdom, and I gave my life to defend my home. I never had that luxury when Loki took my godly life from me. After the release of my soul from the Kraken form, I spent most lifetimes hidden and quiet. I was alone but my focus remained strong although my trust in others had withered. I couldn't rely on mortals with the truth, because if the word got out, he would hunt me using his followers and sometimes even the noble wolves of Valhöll. The past was harsh, but it is not the time to hate.

Secondly, I remembered a more peaceful time in Turkey, when I was considered a Saint. I gifted gold for the dowry of a poor man's three daughters. I also gave small toys to children to play with and enjoy their youth and innocence. Religion was war, a uniformed control that killed or converted. It was as if one list of beliefs had to control the masses, but the children shouldn't have to endure the hardships. Nicholas was my name back then and my purpose was to return the memory of Baldur to the world.

Thirdly, I recalled some of my old writings from when I travelled and lived in Iceland. I was a historian, a politician, and a scholar. I wrote of my time as a god from a human perspective. I tried to explain the complexity of Skaldic poetry and show the similarity of my tales to Christian adaptations. With the old gods far retreated from the minds of men, I had to keep their memory alive. Cryptic clues of an ancient dead language using metaphors and linguistics to explain a deeper revelation. It was something I wrote that helped me remember the location of Vanaheim's entrance.

Time was getting late as I waited for the gods' arrival. I was beginning to think my riddle was too cryptic to decipher. It wouldn't be long before Loki would send more of the Einherjar after me in such a secluded place. Slowly, they emerged from the darkness. My beloved lady Jord, Tyr, Njord and many more gathered on the beach. Each of them dawned their ancient battle armour with weapons sheathed. Now if Loki did send the wolves, they would be slain with ease.

Loki was watching us in all his arrogance and power sat in the heavens. unimpressed and unmoved in the assembly of the gods. However, now that we were attempting to gather a force strong enough to defeat him, he would have to leave his kingdom to squash the attempt.

"Where is my Thor?" Jord asked.

"He will be here when the time is right, my love," I reassured.

"Has he forgiven me?"

"Rest your weary heart, my lady. I shared a drink and feast with him exchanging gifts. He has vowed to rebuild bridges long burned and understands the depth of Loki's deceit. He will come and stand by our sides once more. The time for heroes and gods has returned."

After we discovered the cave, my beloved recited an ancient spell in an old tongue. Her magical incantations made runes appear and illuminate the cave. The breeze picked up slightly, slowly increasing in intensity the further she got into her spell. The gods stood ready with weapons drawn.

Good host, it is always better to be ready for war and never need to fight than have a battle that catches you unprepared. Loki may send werewolves, and he may even send angels, but we would be ready for anything he sends.

My lady finished her spell and moments later a whale breached the surface of the water within the cave. It slowly began opening its mouth. I was wary because I knew my fate. I only planned on entering one animal's mouth and it was only at the right time, the time I had weaved my wyrd. My fate was determined but the time was my decision.

"Come, Aegir and Ran will host us. They will hear our call for aid," Jord's voice drifted delicately. Despite the years of solitude and the bitterness she'd endured alone, her voice still held power over my heart.

We entered the whale's mouth despite the beast's foul breath. Every god, without hesitation, climbed onto the tongue and waited patiently. The whale closed its mouth, creating an air pocket around us. It was dark and damp as we felt the whale descend into the watery abyss. It remained still as it drifted towards Vanaheim.

Deeper and deeper, we descended into the watery lands that have claimed many men and women over the years. The unknown creatures that prey on each other far from the sight of humans but not far enough to remain out of their imagination. Tentacles and teeth, fighting and biting to claim the title of the terror of the seas. They were fighting for second place, as true terror was birthed by Angerboda.

Suddenly, the whale arrived at Aegir's aquatic kingdom. As we disembarked from its mouth, I could catch a glimpse of a vision. A vision of my throne vacant. Loki was on his way, and I didn't have time to leave anything to chance. I had to allow Loki to reveal his intention, while rallying Aegir and the Jotuns to my side. His spiteful words would fuel his enemies to rise against his oppression and control.

An elf stood guard at the entry. He remained poised and unfazed by our presence there. We approached him with weapons lowered or sheathed. Without a word, he allowed us to enter through the giant doors. It had been many years since I had visited Atlantis and I had no idea if we would be welcomed or killed on sight.

The hall echoed and groaned as the slaves set the table and Ran, walked toward Aegir on his throne. As I looked upon Aegir's giant form, I was reminded of times of old when Jotuns had greatness and power that rivalled the gods. He had many slaves that had succumbed to Ran's net. She loved to collect anglers, seafarers and unfortunate souls that found themselves alone on the glassy surface of the ocean. All kinds of beings; the Jotun, the humans and even the elves.

We were seated at the table by the noble elf called Eldir. He left and returned to his guard duty at the door. Our discussions lasted for around three hours. We talked of the hardship Loki's rule has brought to the realms. The misfortune the Jotuns endured during the many years. They were hunted nearly to extinction. It was a world that benefited neither race. Even the humans grow weak calling upon blind faith while Loki's sinister smile lurks in the background. I even cautioned Aegir of Loki's arrival because I knew he could show up at any time.

"He will attempt to promise you a lot in regard to elevating your presence higher, but know this, good Aegir. He has promised peace to everyone and yet more die under an Abrahamic god than any other religion. Witches were burned, werewolves hunted, vampires exiled and even trolls were vilified. Humans have died under the belief they were doing God's work but, they died under Lucifer's justification. He torments the weak by using his followers. He disregards and destroys anything that does not elevate his presence. Loki is smart, cunning, and deceptive but we can win together. We must prepare ourselves and not fall for any emptier promises," I said to rally him and the Jotuns to my side.

Meanwhile, Loki appeared outside and began speaking with Eldir.

"What do the gods discuss over their ale?" Loki asked curiously.

"The Jotuns, elves and gods are conversing over war and weapons. None have any kind words for you."

"Well let me pass and I will squash any uprising they attempt. I will tear this gathering asunder."

"You know, if you enter all your lies and disrespect will simply fuel the gods' cause."

"You know, Eldir. If you and I continue talking, I will be rich in reply toward you."

Eldir guided Loki into the hall reluctantly, apologising for the intrusion. The war council fell to silence, and all stared at Loki as he walked in arrogantly, unafraid of the powerful beings that sat before him.

Without warning, Loki plunged a knife into Eldir's neck. Aegir and Ran rose from their thrones angrily as the gods wanted to take his life then and there. The goal was never to kill Loki, as I had an oath with Heimdall and Surtr. However, he must be brought to justice and his punishment more severe than death. He continued to mock and ridicule the gods without any kind of respect for the hosts.

"I am thirsty, fetch me a drink so I can sit with the gods. Why so silent? Conspiring against me? Give me a seat or send me away," Loki swaggered up to the table.

"You are unwelcome Loki. Leave now! You are not wanted here," Kvasir scolded.

"A long time ago, Odin said I'd be welcome at any table he attended," Loki replied.

"Rise now Vidar, make room for Fenrir's father. I do not wish to be known as one who does not keep his oaths," I instructed as Vidar poured Loki some ale.

"Hail to the gods in all their sacred glory. Hail to all except the one that has been known as Bragi," Loki toasted.

"I'll give you a horse and his cock from my stable. Don't interrupt the gods you're not worth their time," Kvasir responded.

"You will be short of a horse as over the years you have shied away from a fight, Vampire."

"Such a shame Brokkr never took your head for your lies back then. It would have saved us years of enduring your presence," Kvasir snapped back.

"You are brave in your seat but that is all. Silence your tongue or fight now. The brave wouldn't hesitate."

"Quiet now Bragi. Odin's kinship oath still holds. Be silent now, please my love," Idunn soothed Kvasir.

"Silent Idunn! You speak while you wrap your arms around your brother's killer."

"The angry should not fight. Logic fails as rage prevails," Idunn replied.

"Isn't it known that Loki likes a joke or has his humour been lost while he ruled the worlds?" My beloved asked.

"Be silent, mother. Your spirit was seduced when you laid with jack frost and put your thigh over him."

"Foolish you are Loki, to make your mother mad at you. She knows the fate of all, she is Skuld," I told him.

"Remain quiet, Odin! You gave victory to those undeserving. The weak, the pathetic warriors. My Hel gets the strongest of heroes."

"I gave those of worthiest cause victory. At least I never raped anyone to bear offspring. You are an unworthy husband and father, you are a pervert," I replied frustrated with his presence.

"Ah but you too have born children over your many lifetimes. As a witch and a wizard practising Seidr in mortal form. I thought you were the pervert."

"The circumstance you two endured should never be spoken about in front of others. They should be kept distant and regarded as ancient matters," my beloved said soothingly.

"Silence mother! You have always been easy to lay with others. Vili, Ve and Odin's wife."

"If Baldur was still here you would be silenced. There would be no escape from your poisonous tongue," my lady replied.

"Mother, do you wish for me to speak more of my wicked deeds? I ensured Baldur may never rise again."

"You fool! I know of all fates. I choose not to speak it."

"Silence mother! I know you spent time with the dark elves and the Aesir. Brisingaman is evidence of all who hosted you in their beds."

"You lips leak lies. Your time will come. The gods, Jotuns and elves all dislike you. I will cheer as you return to where you belong," my lady scolded.

"Silence witch! You lay with Freyr when he was too old. Such a surprise when you passed wind."

"Foolish Loki, the pervert. That is harmless to care for one's child and comfort him as a young man. You have a large mouth for one with monstrous creatures he no longer cares for," Njord added.

"Be quiet hostage! You find peace with the nine wave-maidens pissing in your mouth."

"It was my comfort far away from Atlantis. I fathered a son that no one hates and has protected the gods," Njord replied.

"Stop now Njord, or I will not keep your secret. It was your sister you had that son with."

"Freyr is the best and boldest of riders. He frees those from aches in the mouth and he makes none cry," Tyr said.

"Silence Tyr! You cannot be truthful, your hand which Fenrir took is evidence of that."

"I've lost a hand, but you've lost your son. He brings pain to us both; it's not pleasant for the wolf in his bonds. He must wait for the twilight of the gods," Tyr said with sorrow.

"Be silent Tyr! Your wife had a child with me. Hödr his name was but I call him Narfi now."

"Your wolf lies before a river, Loki, until his powerful bonds are loosened. You shall share a similar fate unless you hold your venomous words, you fool," Freyr said coming to Tyr's defence.

"A fool that gave his weapon away for love. Your end will come by Surtr, and you will regret you had let go of your only chance of survival."

"Freyr's lineage is my own, Loki. He looks after the youth's teeth which you are causing me to grind mines now," Aegir growled.

"Ah silly Jotun, you come to your grandson's aid as you exist beneath the salty waters grinding your teeth as the stones turned to sand."

"Aegir I am called, and I am too busy to deal with such disrespect. I'm happy the sons of Odin are here together planning your demise," Aegir's voice boomed.

"Be silent Aegir! You never share out food only ale with those you host. You will stay hiding when the gods fight."

"You are drunk with victory, child. Your tongue has become loose the more you're challenged. A fool the wise become when the more success they drink," Heimdall told Loki in hopes to get through to what remained of Freki.

"Best to be quiet Ve! In the past, you had a hateful duty watching over the gods as Heimdall. You must have a bad back old man without a chair to watch over the world."

"You are happy now while you are free but you will be bound by Hödr's intestines," Skadi scowled.

"Ah, the wench speaks. Remember I was present at your father's death."

"You have balls to talk of my father's demise, Loki. At least before the goat got them. Perhaps you have not learned your lesson from so long ago," Skadi glared at him.

"You spoke softer to the goddess of love's son. Remember when you invited me to bed?"

Sif came through the door, returning hope to my soul once more. She walked up to Loki and filled his cup with the rarest of meads. Gently, she placed it in front of him before taking her seat.

"Come now Loki, of all the gods and goddesses I remain blameless," Sif spoke.

"Sadly, it is untrue that you are innocent. I know of another lover besides Thor. It was not I, but Odin that shared your bed."

"The skies rumble amongst the mountains. I think Thor approaches to hush you," Sif said.

"Be quiet whore! Your words are like dung!"

Thor entered boldly through the door. If the room was silent enough, you could hear the skies tremble in his rage.

"Quiet Loki or I shall take your head off with my hammer!" Thor roared.

"Oh, why so angry Thor? You won't be angry when you face Fenrir after he swallows Odin."

"Silence troublemaker or I'll throw you out and you shall never be seen again!" Thor exclaimed furiously.

"Remember our first trip to Thrymir's keep? You ran with your mighty gloves in hand. Some hero you are."

"Maybe I should crush your skull just as I did Hrungnir!" Thor blasted.

"I wish to live for a while yet. You threaten me with your hammer, but it was weak against Skyrmir when you needed food."

"Aaargh Loki! I am going to kill you just like Hrungnir!" Thor yelled as he raised the mighty Mjolnir.

"Okay, I have said what I needed. I know you hit hard, Thor. I shall leave you to your ale brewed and your feast prepared."

Loki left shortly after. His words were carefully used to tear us apart from the inside. Unfortunately for him, it fueled our anger and rage, igniting our passion for war and our desire to dethrone Loki and the so-called saviour, the light, the would-be god. The battle had been set, the armies gathered, and the fuse ignited. The upcoming war would shake the very Skylands. The halls of the gods would be theirs once more.

The Wild Hunt

Soon after Loki's departure, the gods rose from their chairs and raised their weapons, declaring Loki would be hunted down and brought to justice. Some mounted horses, others mounted chariots pulled by goats, cats, and boars. Tyr shed his skin and unleashed his giant bear form. Vali, son of Honir showed a power that reminded me of a time long passed.

He transformed into a werewolf with teeth and claws wrapped in a brown coat. His face stretched and his physique evolved. His senses heightened even further than mine and it would be unfortunate if any mortal saw him in this form. They would never be able to sleep again. He was not like the werewolves of Valhöll, he was more beastly, with glowing green eyes. He was hungry for vengeance for Baldur.

I climbed upon Sleipnir and with my eight-legged Kelpie in reins, we journeyed. Onwards and upwards beyond the mysterious ocean-blue depths. We travelled through the land covered in snow hunting for Loki and those loyal to his cause. Tyr was the best at seeking his prey in the winter, a tribute to his past life when he was Ullr. Now and again, I'd stop into homes that had strong pagan worship and gifted a lump of black coal. Not as a punishment but as a tool to survive the cold harshness winter brings.

All that travelled in the wild hunt were a sight that would terrify some and give hope to others. Some called us ghosts, others called us haunting spirits, but in truth, we were the hunters of Loki and his followers. The echoes of my calls bellowed throughout the skies, "Ho Ho Ho!" to all those that know it was a reminder of how to live. And to those that remained clueless, I was simply a jolly old soul gifting to those that supplied me with cookies and milk.

Humans would tell their children of a time when Santa came with reindeer and elves. Priests would say judgement was coming. In truth, both were right. It was not ours but Loki's and their own God's judgement. For too long they have received praise for greedily claiming power and worship under almost as many names as I.

Allah, Abraham, God, the Messiah and even as the boy that he killed. The boy Heimdall, Honir and I guided as a child, even adopting the form of Jesus, Loki held the hearts of many. Manipulating all to believe that the world could live in peace while destroying her resources, while expanding the population and polluting her beauty. As things are becoming more desperate on the lands because all fight for more gold or an easier life. You can almost feel the chaos of Ragnarök approaching.

We took our steeds, and we travelled high up the mountains, into the lands of Jotunheim. We gathered as many Jotun to our cause as we could because the army of Heaven has the mighty Valkyrie turned into Archangels and they would be the mightiest foes we would ever face. They were warriors that claimed many lives over the years.

Into the skies across Europe, we went leaving shadows and haunting silhouettes amongst the clouds. It was the winter solstice, and the nights grew longer. The thick clouds blotted out the stars. Hope dwindled amongst the lands of men, as not even Mani could give comfort in the darkness that we brought to heaven's gates.

Freyr returned to the hidden city of Alfheim to assemble another mighty army of fairies, elves and other Landvættir to the cause. Three mighty armies to take down one. That was the power Loki and God had. It would take an army of gods, jotuns and elves just to reclaim Asgard from their hands. They were an adversary we had never come across before and we have had many over the years. Jotuns enhanced by Verdandi's magic, even Verdandi herself but none would compare to the foes we were facing now.

As we approached those golden-imbued pearly gates, we were surrounded by a haunting mist. If it wasn't for my godly vision, I would have been as blind as Hödr. We created a phalanx, an impenetrable strategy that showed equal trust to each of the beings within. Each of the gods stepped cautiously toward what used to be our glorious home. We remained silent, thinking we had the element of surprise, but we were wrong.

Suddenly, the gates of heaven crashed open as the former Valkyrie swarmed us. It was time for war. We stabbed our spears and waved our weapons to fight them off. Lightning bolts summoned by Thor caught a few of the feathery-winged warrior maidens. Tyr transformed back into a man and began slashing at the skies with Tyrfing. Heimdall could anticipate the enemy's attacks making them easier to slay using Hed. The battle appeared to be hopeless until a sound of a horn echoed through the clouds.

The sounds of heavy steps rumbled the Skylands as large shadows appeared in the fog. Aegir and Ran had rallied as many of the Jotun as they could. The mountain giants plucked the angels out of the air and threw them to the ground. The trolls and ogres swiped their massive clubs at the few angels that flew low. Yeti, Sasquatch and Yowies all charged bravely toward the battle ending our hopelessness.

A second horn blew. It was richer than the previous horn. The noble elves of Alfheim came to Freyr's aid. Elves, fairies, and warrior nymphs took to arms, united under a single cause. They fought mightily as many fell to the Valkyrie and their weapons. Magic and blood painted the skies red, but we were still headed towards defeat. If this was to be my end or another attempt to make me suffer mortality once more, so be it, I would continue to fight.

All appeared lost until a third horn blew. It was a deeper groan than Alfheim's horn. As I scrambled to find the source, my gaze met my beloved's as she smiled. It was Svartalfheim's dark elves that answered our call for war. My beloved Jord still held the heart and loyalty of creation. After all, we do not create things unless we love to do them. The dark elves, dwarves and goblins emerged through the haunting mist from every dark forest or gloomy cave. For the first time since my brothers and I created the realms, the inhabitants were united.

The Valkyrie had finally met their match. It took an army never seen before in the nine realms. Jotun, gods and elves from all corners of the world tree, all united to remove Loki from my throne. It was a battle that inspired tales all over the lands below. I would have preferred a more peaceful solution but that was never an option with dealing with my sworn blood brother.

The army held the Valkyrie at bay as I gathered myself to seek out the false god. The others fought fearlessly and although many fell it appeared that the tide had turned. We could win this fight and for the first time in many lifetimes, I felt joy once more. Travelling the Skylands, I noticed it had become barren in my absence. The trees and the meadows had lost their beautiful embrace. Asgard rotted as a careless fool that cared for nothing, but power and chaos ruled from above.

I approached Valhöll uneasy with the wreck that was left. An unkept place of residence shows three things. A lack of pride, a lack of care and a lack of respect. You would have had to be blind to remain unaware of the history and glory of my hall to not show it the respect it deserved. I was only a few hundred metres from the entry before I saw a shadowy figure emerge from behind the door. A familiar howl caused me to tighten my grip on Gungnir.

A large beast stood at the doorway. Its fur was thick and as black as the night sky. Beyond its fangs dripping with saliva, its green eyes glowed as it began a low growl. It looked like Vali, only darker in colour and not on our side. My mind raced throughout my history and then I discovered an answer. It lowered to all fours before beginning its charge towards me.

It was quick but with the power of Verdandi, I was quicker. Time slowed, but this beast charged at a speed unfathomable by human eyes. I stood my ground and just as it pounced towards me, my mind was drawn to contemplate my fate. Milliseconds passed like hours but I was said to meet my end in the jaws of a wolf. Was this my end? Was my fate to end here? This wolf was too small to swallow me whole.

Suddenly, the Vali on our side intercepted the one on Loki's. Tooth and claw tore at each of their flesh and fur. A brutal battle of evenly matched brothers took my attention away from Loki for a few moments. It was enough time for Loki to appear from the entrance of Valhöll and cast a Seidr spell on them both. It bound them both together as two halves of the same being.

As they struggled and whimpered, the two wolves combined into an interesting being needed for the next generation to survive. Vali stood up in human form but appeared to be on my side. After lowering my spear, I turned to see Loki's malevolent smile as the door to my hall closed behind him. Vali appeared hungry for victory but also greedy for all the glory to be his and his alone.

"Gather yourself, Vali, and help the others if you can. I have a score to settle with my blood brother," I said as I rushed in towards my Hlidskjalf. I knew I couldn't kill Loki or even spill his blood on Asgard's soil. However, I knew I had to bring him to justice to right a wrong written so long ago.

I burst through the doors but it wasn't who I was expecting that met my gaze. Loki had retreated to leave another to deal with his and their consequences. I was taken back by the god I saw, for I had not seen him in many years. It was my son, Hödr. The boy I taught so long ago. The one I educated in the art of war, physical prowess and combat skill. Hödr stood up from Hlidskjalf and readied his weapon. It appeared that his sight had returned but he remained blind to the plight of his followers.

"Son, I have returned."

"Old man claiming to be my father but what have you given me? Nothing just the ability to fight with no vision to apply it! I may have been your son in another life, but Loki gave me my vision back. He gave me what I needed to rule the heavens!" Narfi yelled.

"Ignorant fool! Loki gave you what he wanted to gain a puppet on the throne. You may have your sight back, but you will always be blind to the truth if you only choose to believe that those who gift you are your friends. I took your sight so you could teach others the lessons you have lived. You were supposed to teach humans that ignorance isn't the path of leadership but innocence can become knowledge."

Narfi started to step toward me. Each step pounded like a slow and confident warrior's heart. "Perhaps it's time to teach you a lesson, Yulefather."

Immediately, Narfi's blade clashed with my spear. I was old but with Kvasir's blood, Verdandi's magic and my knowledge, I out manoeuvred each attack and responded in kind. Blow after blow, I dodged swiftly. Each swipe of his sword sliced through the thick air causing the haunting fog to lift from Asgard. He began panting and gave the occasional roar out of frustration.

I began to decipher Loki's grand plan during the fight. Loki may have begun as God, but he used Höðr to replace him once he fully established a following in Midgard. He turned man and woman away from courage and strength, it all began to make sense to me. He was raising an army far more formidable than the Angelic Valkyrie. Weakening humanity to become puppets in the war to come. I had to regain my throne to find Loki.

I dodged Narfi's forehand slash and pierced his right knee. His agony and aggression echoed throughout my hall. I ducked a backhand strike and pierced his left leg. Narfi's hand dropped his sword as God finally took his rightful place and knelt before me. Höðr was never supposed to rule just like my eldest brother before me. It was Baldur that was supposed to be king after my death. At least that was my oath and I intend to keep it.

The battle for Asgard was won. The Valkyrie seized their attacks and bowed before me. My lady was by my side and the gods had returned. Asgard began to flourish once more as Höðr would await judgement from one whose heart broke when Baldur died. He would receive punishment for believing in someone like Loki and turning the people from the Aesir gods.

As the sun rose on a new day in Asgard, so did hope for the world. Ragnarök was coming but at least the gods and I could fight from the higher ground. We had our home, but we still needed Loki controlled. With him roaming free, we could not relax or focus on our impact on the world. As my first order of business, as king of the gods, Loki would be brought to justice.

Dashing Through the Snow

Moments after our victory, I was joined by the remaining gods, Jotuns and elves. Freyr brought a ham for the Yule feast as a tribute and celebration of uniting together under the hardship of battle. Asgard was ours again, but we still had to find the one who instigated it all. We still had to bring Loki to Forseti for judgement and punishment for killing his father.

I left the feast to sit upon Hlidskjalf once more. It was larger than I remembered yet its warm embrace held a familiar comfort. My throne was mine again and all who shared in the spilling of blood were welcome to feast at any time. Just as I sat upright my vision flashed throughout the nine realms. In a single moment, the rush was intense. If I did not have peace of mind and focus, I would have been overwhelmed with the visions.

My former brother, Vili now known as Surtr was training his army in scorching heat in Muspelheim. Beneath the black sand in the Sahara, he was always training for the war to come. Hel was reigning over the dead, in the cold and icy Niflheim. She gave comfort to those who passed away in sickness and old age. Fenrir's bonds remained strong but the mountains surrounding him were weary with time. It was more of a sign that Ragnarök was nearby.

The people in Midgard were becoming colder and more distant toward each other. Families are not an example of strong kinship bonds like in the past. Friendships are torn asunder by gold, popularity, and selfish needs. The humans have devolved from Askr and Embla as technological advances keep them apart. The world was causing me to weep, as laziness is encouraged and those that push themselves go mostly unrewarded and unnoticed.

As I wiped my tear I stared further through the lands. A few dark elves escaped Svartalfheim and taunted the weak of heart and those absent of courage. It was their prerogative as the humans had vilified them with Christian overlays and tales of demons. They enjoyed making humans believe they were losing their minds. Hiding things, tripping people, breaking objects acting in stealth like a shadow in the night.

Some Jotuns hid amongst the humans in high controlling positions. They became the heads of companies that are ruthless to the world. They even used humans as pawns in their foolish attempt to raise themselves to godlike status. Some kept the old ways alive and dismissed godly-related traditions as rumours and hearsay.

Coming from high up in the mountainous terrains into forests and jungles to prey on those that become unfortunate and lost on their paths.

The elves, fairies, and nymphs also hid in the woods. Enchanted and barely touched by the ever-expanding human population. Only revealing themselves to those blessed with innocence and imagination, whose worlds were still full of magickal wonders. When nature is untouched, it touches your heart and soul to visit places like these. To leave a dwelling so natural and untouched, taking nothing but the memory of visiting such a place is a sign of honour.

Aegir and Ran returned to their ocean kingdom. They had their hall full of drowned servants that Ran collected with her magical net in Vanaheim. Such an amazing land under the glassy blue surface of the oceans. Creatures of all shapes and sizes, all varieties of colours, all living together in a quiet habitat that becomes darker the deeper you go. Our alliance with the realm was strong and when Ragnarök comes, they will be required to wash the world clean of the devastation to come.

The rest of the lands were in chaos, such is the nature of the world not controlled by a pantheon. Through chaos and turmoil, life always finds a way. It never gives up, through hardship and despite adversity, nature will always have victory. Nature overcomes everyone and everything in the end until we build again hopefully learning lessons left previously from the victories and defeats of the ones that have fallen before us.

I shook myself from the distractions to regain focus on my task. I needed to find my deceptively brilliant oath brother. Suddenly, my vision found my target. He was located in solitude. Deep in the heart of a Jotunheim, in a dark familiar forest, Loki had built a cabin with a door in every direction the compass pointed. It was a tranquil place with a stream that flowed only a few metres away.

It was an age since I had been there. The place I tore my eye out in the pursuit of wisdom. The place where I faced my enemy with my brothers by my side. The place where someone I considered kin betrayed me in their selfish need for power. The place where I swore my oath to save me from death. Mimir's well had three occupants through time and the last that coveted the well of wisdom was Loki.

Loki hid comfortably in solitude and silence. He used his magic and mind to craft things throughout the mornings and spent his days fishing by the stream. He enjoyed his quiet and lonely nights by the fireplace, cooking his catch in the darkness as the flames flickered and danced to the sounds of the breeze. He thought that if he lived quietly enough, no one would ever think to look for him near Mimir's well.

After I watched him for three days, I decided it was time to act. The Yule feast of Valhöll had ended as the Yule log had been reduced to embers and ash. The gods had full bellies and thirst quenched, it was now time for justice. Everyone mounted their chariots and climbed upon their saddles. Every god readied their weapons and the glorious calls from the horns of Asgard could be heard throughout the lands.

Through the clouds we travelled, through the snow on Midgard, we dashed. Over mountains, forests, and swamps, we rode for life and justice. Over the deep blue seas of Vanaheim, we rode. We journeyed deep into the heart of Jotunheim hunting for Loki. The wild hunt came to an end as we approached the place of Mimir's well.

This place still held an eeriness of an old dark time where I bet my head long ago. I scanned ahead of our arrival and could see that Loki was still there. By the time we arrived, he seemed to have vanished from sight. He was nowhere to be found, but Loki enjoyed his power and his cunning wit too much to let an opportunity go. He enjoyed elevating himself above all others by trying to make others look foolish in comparison.

The fire still burned, so he couldn't have gone far. Something peculiar smouldered not far from the fire. The ash outline of something burned on the ground, was a clue we had to decipher. Kvasir walked over and began studying it to decipher what it meant. Vali and I rushed ahead into the well but it was vacant, well almost.

"Ah, you have returned Odin," an old and croaking voice surrounded us in the cave.

Vali and I steadied our footing and readied ourselves for a fight.

"Lower your weapons, fools. You wouldn't attack a peaceful and level-headed fellow, would you?" the familiar voice asked.

"Uncle is that you?" I asked curiously.

"Of course it is. Loki kept me here to shut me up. I have suffered in solitude, longing for the splendour Asgard brings. Can you take me with you back to Asgard?"

"Where is Loki, Mimir?"

"He is closer than you think. He watches the gods outside searching for him. He dances and jumps with joy, right in front of their very eyes."

"Another riddle uncle? I should have known." I grabbed his head and secured it to my back before leaving the cave with Vali.

Emerging from the darkness, I looked at the campsite calmly. Looking at the gods, I scanned their surroundings. In the trees, I saw birds but not Loki. In the distance, I searched but no Loki. I thought deeply about what my uncle said while Thor stood with hammer clutched in hand and Tyr with his one hand on the hilt of Tyrfing. Kvasir examined the ashes of what Loki had just burned as Skadi also examined the surroundings for clues to Loki's whereabouts.

Suddenly, I heard a splash in the stream. My gaze instantly looked towards the salmon swimming and jumping against the current. "There!" I called. The gods looked at me and then straight at the river. Thor stood at one end snatching and grabbing at the fish that evaded him. Tyr transformed into his large bear form also trying to clutch at the fish when it came near.

A few moments passed and Loki enjoyed making the gods look like fools when fishing. Kvasir called out, "I have it! It was a net!" Swiftly, he collected some things to repair what Loki attempted to destroy. He tossed the net over to Tyr and he scooped the salmon out of the water. Loki struggled but he knew that his time had come and there was no escape. He kept his guise up, thinking if the gods remained unsure, they would throw him back.

Thor plunged his hand deep into the net, grasping Loki by the tail. He held him so firmly that the tail was squashed in one of the cold iron gauntlets that wield Mjolnir. If Loki changed back to his usual form, his legs would be unable to carry him away. Some believe that is the reason salmon have such narrow tails but unfortunately, salmon are not children of Loki.

"Show yourself Loki! Before I squeeze a little harder and separate your upper from lower," Thor boomed as the lightning and thunder rumbled and flashed in the skies above.

Loki knew Thor never made empty threats, and it was rarer that Thor would not enjoy showing his strength and power. The gods surrounded him giving him no chance for an escape. Suddenly, Loki transformed and pleaded for mercy. "Don't! Please don't! I'm sorry for what I have said and done over the time I ruled. Please can't we just forgive and forget?"

"There is freedom in forgiveness, Loki. But only a fool would forget all the problems you have caused in life. You must answer for your crimes, and it will be decided by the one you affected most," I said barging my way through the crowd of gods.

"Oath brother you can't! We share a bond unlike any other. An oath that ensures my blood is never spilled." Loki protested.

"You betrayed that oath when you plunged a spear into my side as I hung from Yggdrasil. A second time when you killed Baldur and the third is yet to come but he will receive his death soon enough. However, I would be no better if I never kept my part of the bargain. I will not spill your blood or allow any others to do so. Forsetti will pass your judgement as I search my mind for suitable punishment."

Loki's expression sank from his face. He knew that no matter how much he pleaded his case, Forsetti could see the truth. No amount of word weaving, illusion or deception would allow him to escape his judgement. Forsetti lost his father but was a wise god and a great seeker of truth. Hödr would be another that had to face his nephew's judgement. He too was not entirely innocent either in the fall of the gods and king Baldur.

Fimbulwinter

The gods and I dragged Loki limp-legged over the realms and back to Asgard. We took him directly to Glitnir. This was Forsetti's hall which was made from silver and gold. It was the highest hall in all the kingdoms of Asgard. Loki would be brought and placed next to Hödr for judgement. Their fate would be decided with truth and clarity. None would ever dispute the words of Forsetti because in his court there is nothing but the truth. He was a great judge of character and would always say enough so that his decision would never be misinterpreted or twisted into anything else.

"Loki and Hödr. Your day of judgement has come. Hödr, you were foolishly ignorant to be blind enough to align yourself with Loki and kill my father. You trusted someone that has proven on more than one occasion to be deceptive, manipulative, and not willing to keep his word. A trickster that would bargain with his people and steal from his mother. Hödr, you will be killed by Vali, torn to sunder, and sent to Hel. Your soul can at least reunite with your brother and attempt to make peace in the next life. Do you have any final words?" Forsetti spoke slowly and clearly so that none would be confused about his decision.

"With my time on the throne, I tried to be good and giving just like my mother. I tried to remain kind and forgiving, nurturing, and caring, loving and accepting. Why was my rule not enough?" Hödr asked the crowd of gods watching over the proceedings.

"Permission to answer, good Forsetti," I asked out of respect in his hall.

"You may answer, Odin."

"Life is about balance Hödr. You can't be good without knowing evil. You can't keep giving or people lose appreciation for the gifts. Life can't be all kind because nature is not. Forgiveness must be earned not given away freely in the idea of a peaceful life. If you nurture people too much, they are unable to stand alone without you. You care too much, and they end up disappointing. Love is nature but your love was based on their worship. That's why I encouraged the people to follow their ancestors. They have made the path that they walk on today. Your downfall was accepting Loki's aid knowing his selfish desires would only let him come out on top. You left yourself ignorantly vulnerable to his manipulation. That is why good versus evil is too simplistic and not related to how the world works."

Vali stepped forward through the crowd. Boldy, he moved to the centre of the court. The gods stood quietly and watched as he awaited instruction from Forsetti to act. Hödr looked up towards his son and saw a change in him. Hödr was disgusted as he looked upon the creature that stood before him. Vali was more reserved than the half that Loki watched over before. He turned and faced his destiny, unafraid of what was to come. He did not fight; he did not flee. Hödr accepted his punishment and kept his honour, at least in his final moments.

Forsetti nodded as all watched Vali shed his human form. Teeth, claws and fur as black as night revealed his powerful nature. Loki never showed much expression on his face, but his eyes watched everything. He observed the small details, he knew that I was watching too. I studied every action and sign to decipher clues to what was to come. Even in Loki's carefulness, I could see he masked his true intentions.

While the rest of the gods watched Vali approach Hödr, I saw the echo of the past in the future to come. I knew Loki had been a few steps ahead of us over the millennia. First Vali bit down on the neck of Hödr. He fell to the ground with no struggle or sound. As he began choking on his own blood, Vali used tooth and claw to remove the flesh from Hödr's stomach. It was quite a gruesome sight that I and other gods took no pleasure in watching.

As Vali transformed back to his godly form once more, I couldn't help but notice the unusual circumstance he faced as he sent Hödr to Hel. Two wolves combined into one sounded familiar to me but perhaps it was deja vu. Sometimes we can see the failures of our past ripple to cause turbulent waves in the future. If knowledge doesn't govern our lives, we leave chaos to run free and wisdom is lost. Ignorant are those that leave things up to chance or blind luck when wandering through the times of our lives.

"Now Loki. You are the trickiest of beings. My father took your seat on the council and defeated you when you tried to claim Asgard for yourself. You failed to accept Odin's choice of Baldur as a successor and desired the power of control through half-truths and illusions. You will suffer a fate that keeps Odin's blood oath in place. Your blood will not be spilled, and your death will not come swiftly. You will have to endure tortures of both the mind and body. Tyr's former wife, Sigyn, will share in the punishment for her lack of loyalty to her marriage. Take the intestines of Hödr as intelligence may only be bound with ignorance. Skadi will fetch and secure Jormungandr above Loki. His venom will drip slowly and cause great pain and torture for Loki. Sigyn will be bound by duty to Loki and there all three will stay until Ragnarok comes," Forsetti declared.

An uneasy silence fell in the hall. The sky lands were haunting that day. Loki's punishment was precise and severe. We dragged him in silence to Jotunheim. We found the deepest and darkest of caves. The sun could not penetrate the darkness there. The rocks were the giant teeth of Jormungandr. Entering the dreaded jaws, the gods remained silent as Skadi used her might and magic to keep the sea dragon's mouth open.

Vali took the intestines of the deceased Hödr and began securing Loki to the rocks. Skadi approached simply to watch and smile as Loki received his sentence. My Frigg used a spell to encase both the serpent and Loki in the rocks within the cave. Jormungandr's fangs turned into stalactites and began building in poisonous moisture from his venomous sacks. Just as rock, stone and the chains crafted from Hödr's digestive system enchantingly began to take hold of Loki, he cursed the gods. "You may have me trapped, but when I am free, I vow it'll be the day of your judgement!"

Slowly, the venom began building as Loki lay beneath secured to the rocks. A single drop could melt the very ground, burning like acid. One drop missed Loki by centimetres but the sizzling sound surrounded the cave as Loki began squirming in fear. First, he pleaded more but seeing our actions unwavering, he felt like not even his crafty tongue could aid him in his escape this time.

Another drop fell and landed on flesh. His screams of pain tortured the very soul of his mother, and the earth shook as she turned from her son. My Frigg knew Loki had to receive his punishment for everything he made the gods endure over the years, but it still gave her no pleasure. A mother will always love their child but seeing them suffer and endure punishment is hard on their heart and goes against their very soul. As time waned, the gods retreated from the cave and returned to their lands.

Only my beloved and I remained watching Loki squirm and suffer. It was hard for even me to watch the gruelling punishment, but I stayed to console my lady. Another drop fell on his face and the sizzling only lasted a moment before the screams of anguish took over. Jord trembled again as I wrapped my arm around her and guided her out of the cave. None remained other than the three sentenced, but I returned with one last gift for my oath brother.

"Skål!" I said revealing a larger-than-normal bowl from my sack.

"Bowl? What am I supposed to do with that?" Loki asked.

"Sigyn, take it. You may provide him with some relief for a time and in doing so reduce the hardship on my beloved Jord. You were unfaithful to Tyr but let us teach you the duties of loyalty to your new lover Loki. He had victory over us gods, may you share in his reward," I said sarcastically.

We returned to our halls, not to celebrate or rejoice, but to simply exist and influence the world regarding balance and inspiration. I watch all from Hlidskjalf, including Loki. I use my position to sway the minds of men to honour and wisdom. Loki's influence still exists in the world today, as does Hödr's, but perhaps we Aesir gods and goddesses may have enough time to enlighten all that has been affected by what has already been done.

I don't know exactly when Ragnarök will come, all I know is the more chance I have to sway the battle, the more I can ensure my oath to my son is not broken. There will come a day when the sun sets in the wolf's jaws. There will come a day when my reign as king will be over. And when that day comes, I hold on to hope with honour that the next generation has life and the will to live.

Moving on from that dark day, now is the moment to explain a time you are experiencing at the present. A time when survival takes over everything else. It currently is a time when selfishness will rise, and the innocent will die. A time when an eye for an eye will leave the world blind. The cold is in the air now, can you feel it? People turn on one another, families turn on each other all for riches and the promise of an easier life. If you feel this situation arises, the time for wandering has arrived.

In truth good host, all things that come to an end share the same similarities as Fimbulwinter and Ragnarök. If the three "seasons" become cold and harsh, leaving only memories of great struggle and anguish, then the battle to break free is the only option. Whether it is a job, a lover or a friendship approaching its end, all becomes harsh. The past will be a cold and distant memory. The present is a constant struggle to survive and the future, no matter how victorious you are, looks bleak.

When the signs start to indicate the end, it might be a sign of self-discovery being the only cure. However, even when life is lingering towards its fate, be sure to celebrate the achievements you have reached. The lives you've inspired, the youths you have guided, and the lovers you have shared in a warm embrace. The long summer days that are filled with joy and the cold long nights you have endured because, in the end, they have brought us to where we are today.

So let me describe the time when the world is ending. When humans or opportunities fight and kill to hold on to what little they have left. When the cold forces them to shelter and retreat to survive becoming a victim of a frozen heart. When only your own arms are available to give you comfort. When the friction of your hands is all the magic you can muster as you attempt to warm yourself by the fireside. Clutching onto life and what little hope you have, whether it be a log or a lump of coal that burns, even hope for survival dwindles in the end.

Imagine a time when the path you take is frozen solid and the sunlight is dimmed by thick clouds. A time when the days grow darker. A time when every moment you realise how lonely and cold you are, your very core shivers and shakes like earthquakes. This, good host, is Fimbulwinter. Families are divided, kinship is broken, and the heart grows weary. Just as my mother, Urd, told me long ago this would identify the onslaught of Ragnarök.

Fathers will slay sons, and sons slay fathers. Brothers will scramble and squabble to the death just to hold on to the little of life that remained. In the end, it would be for nothing all will succumb to the doom that lurks amongst the snow and blizzards.

The first season of Fimbulwinter would show itself to be brutal. The few that survive the trials of the cold would be covered in shame by what they did to accomplish such survival. Their honour will be lost for the sake of grasping the little success they have for the rest of their life. When enduring winter, darkness with sustenance scarce, life as we know it wilted.

The second season of Ragnarok will loosen the bonds of Gleipnir. Loki's imprisonment and suffering will cause his mother, my beloved, to shake and tremble greatly. The very world will shudder so severely that the three mountains to which Fenrir is bound will crack and loosen their power over the great beast. Gleipnir will lose its magical hold on the enormous creature and the rise of the Hel hounds.

At first, Fenrir will release a few of the dead werewolves that I slew after they were sent to kill me from my hall. Great warrior wolves were sent to hunt the remainder of the survivors of the great winter. In darkness they would sniff the scent of the living and hunt them down, staining the snow red with blood. They will be good at what they do because of their training at Valhöll combined with being empowered by rage and regret. They will be deadly accurate in their hunt for those that remained alive.

After all that remained is dead, the undead werewolves will return to aid the escape of my adversary with no success. By then, it will be too late to accomplish anything more and it will also be time to keep our heads up, facing the fate that time and our own choices have woven for us. The gods and warriors will turn their back on those that have lived in the world or so it would appear. I will have one last time I leave Hlidskjalf behind and leave the comfort of Valhöll over my shoulder. I will descend from the peaceful world I had reclaimed from God, in the hope to give the next life two hopes and a leader to rule.

Down into Midgard, I will go, through the blizzards and snow. Walking over the land frozen so cold, with only life and the will to live to hold. Whether they are someone you know or descendants years from now, I will keep them from the wolves. I will take them and hide them beneath Yggdrasil herself, to gift hope to those that will rise from the ashes. A gift to inspire and ignite the fire and give you the drive for a world you desire. Leif and Leifthrasir will be the Askr and Embla for the next generation of gods to rise to the throne.

Whether you call me by my names, or by my features or titles, life is not to be a recital. I am Odin, the Yule father or Santa, the father of Christmas, whichever you please. I'm not a god that wishes you to live on your knees. I will hold onto hope with honour and keep my word, my promises and my oaths are all that I am worth. For that is the mark of one that is honourable. One who keeps their word and honours their oaths, even when vulnerable.

After I locate Leif and Leifthrasir I will hold them with care, I will keep them hidden deep in Mimir's lair, they will survive the war to come, when my time is over, when I am officially done. I do this not to be selfish you know; my time might end but my children and grandchildren will rise once more. I do it so that the next generation will have a reason to continue. That is what any parent or grandparent should want when their moment of doom approaches. We do what we must whether it be seen as good or bad, the game of life rarely leaves you glad.

We try our best to teach them wisdom and to make their own judgements. Look at our past, to see our actions in the present as the steps towards the future fast approaching. We try our best in life that is too complex for instruction. Dealing with our own emotions is a big enough challenge but being wise enough to deal with others proves to be even more puzzling. Fate as it seems has already been written. Our life and our choices only dictate the timeline of the death we are already destined for.

The truth about life is that it is all perceptual. It is created by responses to circumstances. Some rise to the challenge while others fall. Every direction we take is like planting a tree. Rooted in the past and branching out towards the future. Tend to it carefully, water it regularly and feed it from the joyous sun and watch it grow like a world of your own. Whether it be a family tree or an extended olive branch for friendship, our worlds cannot flourish when we stand alone.

Our worlds are full of opportunities, emotions, solutions, and creations that will build and destroy all you hope for. Such is life good host. Do you know why it is better to realise you are only middle-wise? Because only I know all. I know everyone's history; I see everyone's actions in the present and I can predict their future based on probability and outcomes. Could you handle that burden? Always calculating and constructing plots. Life is seldom peaceful for those that rule like I, good host.

I am not perfect but never claimed to be. I have started wars and caused struggles because I am ambiguous about life itself. I lead my kin when I can, but they rule themselves with minimal guidance. Sure, I have handed down what I could in terms of lessons and wise words, but guidance is the best of gifts. Not to instruct because there are many paths to take to the top of many mountains. Each of my children and my children's children were raised for a purpose. Beyond my life, they must survive into the next.

After I return from Mimir's well I shall use the power of the runes to guide them through their lives. Honir will receive the mark of Hagalaz. Vidar will receive the mark of Mannaz. Magni will be marked with Thurisaz and Modi with Tiwaz. The third final mark will go to Vali, and it will be the cause of adaptation in the next life. He will receive Laguz. Like war paint with power, the runes gift just enough direction to indicate the future to come.

Search the Elder futhark, each letter is a mark for identification. Search them for guidance and use them for affirmations to direct my children to their fates. Look to the runes then you will know what to leave your children when your time ends. I have three more letters to gift; I swore an oath on one and the other mark will go to his brother. The one that was slain to imprison Loki. The third mark is to right wrong not written by my own hand.

Sometimes blame is placed upon us by the deceptions of others. Stories exist told from the perspective of others and sometimes fighting the lies directly is a wasted battle. Sometimes making amends is looking toward the future and accepting the past can't be changed.

My beloved currently endures the suffering of Loki's punishment. When the time comes, she will break the stones, where Hödr's intestines hold Loki. In doing so she will also shatter the mountains that surround Everest.

Deep within the belly of the beast, the mighty ship called Naglfar will be manufactured. The ship will be made from the nails and toenails of those accepted in Helheim. This is the reason why the bodies of the dead were presented to Hel with care and respect. The reasoning behind their manicured and respectfully dressed appearance. An honourable send-off but another tactic to slow the progress of Ragnarök creeping closer.

Silent Night

In the future, Loki's continued torturous suffering will shatter the mountains with deep roots. The mountains which Gleipnir is secured, and my nemesis is held. Each drop of venom will shake the very foundation of Yggdrasil. Fenrir will, one day, be free from the bonds that hold him. Angry and vengeful he will bring the two gods behind his imprisonment ever closer to their fate.

Höðr's guts will not hold Loki forever and he too will break the bonds which hold him. Once free, Loki will aid his serpent child from the rock holding him in place. Releasing Jormugandr, he will spray poison throughout the lands and destroy the nature of the world. For so long Loki suffered from his own child's venom but to challenge the gods he will require help. The mighty Thor is a powerful foe that Loki needed an ally of equal strength in the battle to overcome.

Jormungandr will cause famine destroying even the trees that remain unaffected by the cold harsh climates. The serpent would be the first horseman of the apocalypse to be released from his prison. Pestilence will wither and wilt the world of its beautiful nature. Loki will continue his journey towards Tibet, under the guise of one that he installed into his religion. He will shape-shift into Jesus to seek the one that is destined to kill me.

Once Loki locates the wild wolf reduced to a dog in chains, he will gain an ally in the son he helped imprison. After many lies and an empathetic apology, Fenrir will doubt him at first, but revenge can be quite persuasive to one so angry. Loki will promise justice for the gods, which will speak to Fenrir's desire. In return for the wolf's aid, Loki will be granted safe passage to Helheim to meet another.

Entering the jaws of the colossal Fenrir, where the river the gods call Thund flows, Loki will journey to the heart of the beast. There, he will barter and bargain with his beautiful daughter. Hel will have her reservations at first, but Loki has a very cunning tongue. He will lie to her that it was Odin that convinced Höðr to rape her, a misleading lie. He will then sell his point by stating that it was him that was responsible for sending the bold Baldur to her side and ensuring he stayed with her. He gifted her love as recompense for her treatment. Hel will not only gift him an army she will also ensure Baldur does not take part on the battlefield called Vígríðr.

After his council, he will depart the heart of Fenrir and descend into the belly of the beast. There he will taunt Nidhoggr a little more before being consumed and sent to Muspelheim. There he will meet his other biological father and my former brother, going by the name of Surtr. Surtr will have his horde of fire Jotuns at the ready with his mighty blade holstered by his side. My brother has been patiently waiting for millennia to set fire to all I hold, and with Loki's aid, he can have what he desires most.

Loki will then climb from Nidhoggr's throat, enraging the beast to break free from the roots of Yggdrasil, which have held him for so long. Once free, Nidhoggr will complete his path to where the army from Jotunheim can travel towards the greatest war in the history of all lands. Loki will climb through Fenrir and up to his mouth. There he will pull Tyr's sword from his lower jaw removing the beast from its bonds and burden.

As the mighty wolf shakes itself free from the silken ribbon, he will howl so loud that Sol and Mani will stop in their tracks. Fearing the horror Loki has unleashed onto the world, each of the beautiful elves will turn and face their mighty persuers. Fenrir will stand in Midgard as his head is above the clouds watching his offspring in a mighty battle with Sol and Mani. Loki will have released the final two horses of the apocalypse. Fenrir will be the slayer of the gods of war and Hel will stand idle as death.

The battle in the skies will begin. Sol will fight valiantly and succeed in slaying her foe. Unfortunately, Mani will fall never to rise in the darkness again, but in doing so ignite a warrior's fire in Sol until she slays the other wolf out of the sky. Weak and wounded from the battle I will quickly collect her child and store her with Leif and Leifthrasir in Mimir's well. She too shall survive into the new world. She will be as gloriously beautiful as her mother and strong like her mighty father, Suttung. Her name will be Sunna.

After seeing his children fall, Fenrir will convulse and regurgitate the army of Hel for Loki to lead. The army will be in the hundreds of thousands and the undead Draugr will march. Each step will beat the earth like a mighty war drum as they approach the battle. Fallen warriors as far as my all-seeing eye can see. Jotun warriors of monstrous size snarling and growling amongst them with weapons drawn and armour fastened.

When Fenrir is finished unleashing Loki's army, he will lose some of his colossal size. Composing himself, the mighty wolf will jump high into the sky and with snapping jaws will devour Sol and the sun causing the dreaded wolf to regain his great size once more. Fenrir will bring the lands to an uneasy twilight and his howl will herald Loki's army like a black rooster. His call will alert the gods of Asgard to come to the battle.

The gods of Asgard, the elves of Alfheim and the glorious warriors that were chosen will march to our doom. The Valkyrie will fly across the skies like a flock of ravens hungry for the aftermath of the battle to come. My armies will bravely head towards our end, to Vígríðr, our final battlefield. With no doubt in our minds, we will march. The echoing sound of the Gjallarhorn will ring, and Heimdall will call like a golden rooster. As the doors of the halls open and with the warriors that remain, we will march.

From Valhöll to Folkvang, the Valkyries will fight, the wolves will fight, and all the godly halls will empty. Bilskírnir, Himinbjörg, Glitnir and Nóatún will empty, and all will march towards the greatest war that the world will ever know. The twilight of the gods will come and what a glorious battle it will be. The sound of clashing steel and splinter shields will fill the air. Magic enchantments, monstrous roars and blood-curdling screams of pain will echo.

Three will remain behind to defend Asgard. My beloved, her son Freyr and the one who he sacrificed his sword for. They will be all that stand against the fire Jotuns of Muspelheim when they come to Asgard's lands. They will fight with courage, strength, and love. They will use whatever weapons they can muster in Asgard's final battle.

Freyr will draw an antler from his helmet, just as he did against the wall builder. The fight with Surtr will be glorious and tragic. The Jotun's large fiery sword will cut through the sky like a solar flare. Freyr will dance and avoid such blows, until he is eventually struck down never to rise again.

His lover will fall next, as the support of love dwindles. When the golden boar armour slowly loses its shine, then the foundation of love will rise to face the Fire giants of Muspelheim. My beloved, my lady, my Jord will use her might and magic to defeat my brother's onslaught. Consumed by earth, Surtr's horde will fall like embers from a volcanic ash cloud. The ashes of the army will fertilize the ground with stories of fools with power and why they should never abuse that gift bestowed on them. Then the queen of Asgard will take a knee, exhausted by the victory in battle.

The battlefield will fill up with Jotuns and undead warriors that have departed from the monstrous ship, Naglfar. They will flood the battlefield marching behind Loki. The crunching of bones and clinking of armour will be deafening with their great numbers. Loki will also have two of his children to fight by his side as Hel watches from Helheim with Baldur by her side.

Why will Hel not take part in the fight? Well, it is to do with my son refusing to fight against his kin. He has seemed to charm her in his time in Helheim and because of his refusal, she must watch over both him and Höðr. It was all part of the fate I could see. Everything began unfolding because of the careful placements and guidance I gave in the past.

Before I lead the gods, the elves, the Valkyrie, and the glorious champions of Midgard, I will consult Mimir. Secured to my waist and ask him one question. "Did I do enough?" His reply will be both a harsh reality and a truthful realisation.

"You cannot ask another at your end if you have done enough in your lifetime. Only you will know. If your energies were focused on what to leave behind when you are gone, that is all that matters. A memory, a great story full of wonder and awe. Your life has been a journey that not all will understand, but if you kept oaths despite the difficulties you faced, glory will be yours. if you inspired your children's victories or taught them humility in failure, then your journey will have been one of worth. No one is perfect in this life, and even if for a time you were, others' perceptions will not allow it to remain so. Death is the lottery of life. If you invest it in precious moments, your time of death will be exactly what you win. People will miss you, but your kin will allow you to live on through their memories."

Ragnarök

When no other options are available, then war is the only answer. The armies of Hel, Jotunheim and Muspelheim will gather on one side and those from Asgard, Vanaheim and Alfheim will stand shoulder to shoulder across the field. Warriors as far as the eyes can see, battle roars will echo. On one side, Fenrir's large size casts a great shadow over the great gap between. Jormungandr also stands imposing his terror from Loki's side of the field. His fangs dripped as Thor's thunderous clouds and flashes of lightning will light up the darkness.

The rotting corpses from Helheim will leave a damp and foul smell of death in the air. Their pale dead eyes will stare at us lifeless through the darkness, but our hearts will remain unafraid. Their bones wear what remains of flesh that is left like tattered rags on a homeless person. These Draugr will have a little more fight in them than those from a previous time. More organised, more structured under Loki's command at the will of their noble queen.

Amongst the dark clouds, flashes of reds and oranges will appear as Nidhoggr will cast a great shadow over the field. He will soar amongst the clouds, indifferent to each side readying for war below. The time for the greatest battle this world will ever see will arrive and the twilight of the gods will be a glorious end to my rule. Protecting and fighting for something more than themselves, my allies and kin will bring me great joy in my final moments. Going to battle selflessly to ensure the next era has the best opportunities to thrive.

Tyr will turn towards the warriors on our side and tell the most inspiring words you will ever hear. "As we look at the overwhelming numbers of our enemy, we stand together. Our hearts are forged with steel and our unshakable will. Take it from me, mighty elves, warrior wolves and Valkyrie. You cannot have glory without bravery. If you fall on this day, be sure to take as much of them with you as possible. I will fight with you not as a god of glory or bravery, but as a brother. FOR THE GLORY OF ASGARD!"

This will stir up passion in each of the warriors that stood by our side. This will be the driving force behind each swing of the weapon. The werewolves will howl in unison, the Valkyrie will screech and caw, and the elves will clash sword against shield. The mighty war drums will ring as Loki will look over with his burning green eyes, confident with his force's numbers and strength.

I will be next to drive my army to victory. "Warriors of Asgard, my wolves, my ravens and my kin! You have fought for millennia, honing your skills and abilities.

The enemy may outnumber us nine to one, but I will always choose the noble and the honourable. Each of you with me now have inspired many, achieved much and ascended above the rest. We have shared stories, feasts and mead. The size of the dog in a fight does not matter. What matters is the size of the fight in the dog. Tyr, do what you can to slay your former friend. He has your arm best take one of his legs as a gift for a gift. I and Vidar will follow you, my boy. That beast won't stand a chance. Thor, you wanted Jormungandr, you got him. Crush and grind his skull with the mighty Mjolnir. Heimdall, I can't kill your child, only you have the right to do so. He's cunning but you've defeated him before, use your Hed. Everyone else, fight! Not for me, but so your names will echo into the next life. So, your stories will not be ash when the flames come. THIS IS WHERE WE STAND! THIS IS WHERE THEY DIE! HOLD ON TO HOPE WITH HONOUR! FIGHT WITH ME NOW BROTHERS AND SISTERS AND DEATH WILL BE YOUR GLORY!"

The ground will shake and tremble as the feet of warriors march. The skies will rumble as gods face monsters and heroes face the Draugr. The world will weep red as the corpses begin to pile up. The warriors from every realm will meet each other with tooth, blade, and claw.

Tyr will run at a great pace first transforming into a large bear to meet his former ally. Just as he meets his foe he will transform back into a mighty warrior and with Tyrfing take the beast's right paw. He will dodge snapping jaws and razor-sharp teeth simply to take that of equal value to the gift Fenrir took so long ago. Sadly, Fenrir will claim the god of war's life. The behemoth beast will throw his corpse to the side of the battlefield and turn his gaze towards me.

I will ride my sleigh pulled with my Kelpie, Prancer. Just when the beast's eyes meet mine, I will take my last moments in this world and look to fulfilling my oath to my son. I will ride swiftly to my fate and enter my nemesis's open mouth. Down the jaws, I will go, towards the heart of the beast. Vidar will follow in close succession, keeping the gateway open. He will hold the jaws open so that three may make their escapes.

Reaching the heart of Helheim, I will find my two sons near the well where Hel looks over the battlefield. It will be deathly quiet, and the air will be damp. This place will no longer be accommodating as it once was. It will be darker, harsher, and cold. It will feel like despite being another realm, Fimbulwinter will have transformed its very reality. I will approach my two sons, Hödr and Baldur, and reach into my large sack for a gift. I will give Hödr Sumarbrandr and Baldur Gungnir. I will also paint a Rune on each of their heads. Othala will be on Baldur's and Wunjo on Hödr's. They will be my last two gifts to the new world, or at least that's what I thought.

They will now have the means and the weapons to leave Helheim behind them. They will escape through the opening that Vidar will hold strong as I remain behind. From the shadows, Hel will appear hurt and angry towards me. She will approach me in a threatening manner and then I will also gift her. Nothing like a gift to right a wrong, even if it was not your mistake to correct. I will breathe life into her decaying face and restore her beauty to its full glory. The life in my face will drain and wither as a result of the sacrifice I will give.

After catching her reflection in the blade of her weapon, she will break down into tears. She will weep because Baldur is gone, and she'll never be free from her duties over the dead and the Draugr. I will console her gently and raise her to her feet. "Here is my gift to you, little girl. I will take over your duties in this place and you shall be free to live in the new world," I will say cheerfully as I paint the rune Jēra on her head. Unfortunately, she would have to wait to be rescued from another, but she will and she will be as lovely as my lady was the first time we locked eyes.

During this time, Vidar will have torn Fenrir with a larger smile, ripping the lower jaw from the upper and piercing the heart with a sword to free Baldur and Höðr from their time in Helheim. The mighty beast shall fall, never to rise again. The warriors from Asgard will cheer in the glory of Vidar's massive victory over the colossal enemy but will swiftly return to fighting the horde of undead Draugr.

Meanwhile, Thor will be slaying Jotuns by the hundreds, dropping them with each swing of Mjolnir. This is why I delayed his fate when he fished for Jormungandr. If I hadn't cut the line forcing him to miss, he wouldn't be at the final battle to slay the Jotun enemy. The battle will almost appear in our favour until Loki sends his serpent son to join the fight. Jormungandr will slither past foes crushing and consuming them on his way to his final face-off with Thor.

Lightning will flash and thunder will roar as the hero of Asgard delivers deafening blows. The mighty thunderer will stand glorious above his nemesis, as the serpent will clutch to the remainder of his life. Thor will approach the weakened serpent and smile. Raising his hammer high in the sky, Thor will bring it crashing down on the snake's head, grinding its skull into the earth. The glorious cheers of my warriors and kin will echo throughout the world.

However, Thor's fate will be met when a cloud of venom and toxic gas will surround Thor. He will grasp at his throat and struggle for breath. Mjolnir will drop from his hand, never to be raised by his again. Unsteady on his feet, Thor will take his final nine steps, just like my father in the battle with Ymir and fall forever. Silence will fall on the battlefield as even the mighty succumb to death. Loki unaffected by the loss of his two sons will smile at the carnage he will cause.

Honir will slay many Draugr on his way to cross blades with Loki. Unfortunately, the estranged brothers will fight each other only to be stopped by their father. Loki will better Honir, but just before Loki attempts to slay him, Heimdall will block the finishing blow. Tyr's former sword will clash with Heimdall's, and the sparks will fly. Loki and Heimdall will be locked into an epic duel, only to fall by each other's hand. Just as Heimdall says his final words of the gods victory, the forked-tongued Loki will hiss and refuse to believe he has lost.

As all the corpses lay dead on the battlefield, the gods of Asgard, warriors of Alfheim and allies in Vanaheim will rest in peace knowing they were victorious in their death. Baldur, Hödr, Honir, Vali, Vidar, Magni and Modi will find refuge in Mimir's well, finding a boat to save them from the flood to come. Baldur, Hödr and Honir will recover Leif, Leifthrasir and Sunna to begin the world again. The stories of gods and heroes will live on through the memory of the survivors as they take on their own challenges in the new world.

Nidhoggr's shadow will circle the dead below. He will swoop over the field to collect the corpses in his wings before heading to Asgard. Weighed down with the corpses, he will slowly struggle to fly through the clouds. This will provide enough time for Surtr's blade to scorch the land via my beautiful and beloved lady Jord. This will give enough time for the Skuld to become Urd in the new world as time flows in the ever-cyclical nature as it does and always will. The past affects the present and the present challenges you to write your future.

Reaching the sky lands, Nidhoggr will face my beloved in a battle of flame and earth magic. The rattling bones from the corpses draping from his wings allowed my lady to gather herself for one final fight. The earth will be ash and the skies will burn as the earth will no longer belong to my lady. I gifted that power to another so my Frigg could become something more.

The great dragon will exhale a burning blaze that will surround Jord. While her skin is scorched, the remaining lands left will be turned to ash. However, my wife is a Norn and as time burns her, she gains a new power as the rune Ūruz will appear glowing beyond the flames. She will become Urd and sent a spell to the sky to summon an old ally of mine. The past will always be a tool to use when we fight our final battles, and our future is no more.

Suddenly, the north star high above Yggdrasil, the star on the yule tree, will begin to dance in the sky. It will fly gracefully as it once did when it pursued me. Suttung, the glorious Phoenix, will soar towards Asgard for his final fight. The dragon's breath will be useless against the fiery bird and will burn and disintegrate the Nidhoggr's wings and the corpses draped from them. With the dragon grounded it shall engulf the noble bird in a single bite. With Nidhoggr in its weakened state, Jord will use the last of her earth magic to trap the beast in a volcano once again.

With Jord burned, Njord and Skadi also gained runes. Ansuz on Njord and Raido on Skadi. Both together shall flood the earth, sinking it beneath an ocean. All the land will sink beneath the surface of the floods, while the remaining gods will scramble for survival. In their struggle, Skinbladnir will conveniently drift across the surface. My widow, now turned Urd, will rescue the gods from drowning.

And then my time will have come to an end. I will watch from Helheim as it will be my new home. The new world will continue in my absence. Nothing lasts forever, good host, not even me. All I can hope for is that I've inspired enough in my children, and my friends, so that at least a story of a god far outlives my predecessors.

Like I said before, good host. The magic of memory is what makes everything I do worth remembering. Even a god will be an ancestor of other gods one day, hence why I act accordingly. Genetics passed down to my offspring ensures my magic lives throughout my bloodlines. Imagination inspired the creation of my story. For the inspiration of my kinship and to show the benefit of honouring a promise. I aspire to inspire those that believe in me and my kin. Everything I have done; I did for love.

Happy Yule (War is over)

When the dust settles by the oceans flood, and deep beneath the waves, lies the mystery of what once was. A life, a history of a world that you may have seen on the surface, but the truth of life is rarely so easy to understand. Were there things I could have done better? Should I have ignored my oath to Loki and his fathers? Well, if I had, it wouldn't have made me very honourable, would it?

I don't claim to be perfect or all that is right in the world. Perfection is an unrealistic attainment, even from a god's perspective. A god rarely cares about such things, even evolution doesn't care about perfection. If anything, I am just a father that tries to lead his world, managing his opportunities when he can. I deal with emotional chaos as it presents itself, trying to remain humble about my accomplishments.

Although the glorious have experienced success, the wise know that there may be failure on the horizon. Failures are not just obstacles to success, but the journey legends must take when living their lives and writing their stories. No story worth telling never had the hardship of failure, and no heroic tales lasted centuries because all was good. They became memorable through the hardship of impossibilities overcome. Mountains climbed, monsters faced, and a life well wandered, that is the story that many are willing to share. Epic tales inspire those to achieve more. Stories enhanced with mythological monstrous metaphors to change a human from a myth to a legend.

A life of memories ascends to an ancestor with genetic links to those in the past and future. Imaginative and creative with kin by their side. The aspiration for something to leave behind for their children and maybe even their children's children. All are done with the power of love, which is learned from their life partner. It is the magickal seed that drives us to create our world tree. A life rooted in the past but that which also branches out to the future.

The life we create can be related to a tree in the forest. Our past must tend and water the roots through the rain and bad weather. Our present provides challenges to grow through. The joyous sun keeps us growing at different rates against other trees in the forest. Our future is to stand tall and strong, unmoved by the gusts of problems that may attempt to blow into our life. The different seasons of the year may appear to mimic your glory and downfall. In spring you come back from hardship. In summer you flourish, in autumn you wither and in winter you endure only to flourish again. Life is complex but nature has a way of explaining it in some cases.

What happens in the next life you ask? Whatever foundations you create for the next generation. Your legacy will inspire those to achieve or surpass what you have done. Maybe they will or maybe they won't but that is their journey of life. Once you are gone you have no power to change things. You simply may just inspire or be remembered as a poor example. Either way, you can only hold onto hope with honour and be a memory of times long past.

It's funny usually people send me letters of what they want for Yule and my final gift for everyone before I died was letters. Letters to guide others in the next life, a declaration of my oaths and will. The runes I used to tell my stories, share my poems, and share what I have learned over my many years as a god, a human and a monster of another religion.

The letters I gave to the next generation were a guide from times long past. An ancestral gift from historical times with meaning and inspiration. A lot can be put down to having a good name in terms of fame, fortune, and strength. A name can inspire you to seek its origin and uncover someone else's story. It is an honour that has lasted through the ages.

Baldur's rune, Othala, will guide him in the next life when he becomes the new Odin, the leader of the gods. His brothers in the war, Hödr and Honir, will become Vili and Heimdall, guided and taught by Vidar as the new Mimir. My beloved and my lady, will become Urd as the new Verdandi and Skuld must be discovered. Magni will find and wield his father's weapon, becoming the new Thor and Modi, his brother, will become Tyr.

Vali's duality you have witnessed before and should now understand the need for the complex nature he will have. The balance of desire between greed for everything and a hunger that can be satisfied. The Laguz rune will allow him to become the new Loki, blood oath brother to Baldur in the next life. Be cautious good host, intelligence has its part in life, but it should never be allowed to rule above knowledge and wisdom.

Njord and Skadi, after flooding the world, will become Aegir and Ran. These Jotun rulers of Vanaheim will also find and adopt a beautiful daughter. One that I gifted three things; a chance of freedom, the chance to find love and the rune Jera. That daughter will become the new Jord and the rest, well, that will be Baldur's story to tell.

When Baldur discovers the new challenges that love and leadership provide, he will uncover the pieces of an ancient game called Tafl, not unlike chess. Baldur will be the new king and each piece of the puzzling game shall have a god or goddess linked to it. The gods of the next generation will play the game of life in hopes of better success in their victory when their version of Ragnarök ends.

Life can be like a game of chess, good host. Some people you meet will be pawns, others are knights. You are the king and the one that manoeuvres them all in the hope of victory. The more enemies moves you can predict and counter, the fewer the chances you can lose. Sometimes it may take the sacrifice of the queen for a time, but you should always try to have one as it is an advantage on the battlefield of life. Different pieces move in different ways, but remember your enemies have the same pieces that move in the same way. Be aware of all pieces on the board before making your move.

In the end, all I can hope for is that my children and grandchildren play the game of life a little better than I did. Isn't that the true meaning of life? To wish that others aspire to be like you but also to do it a little better. Well, that is the meaning of my life isn't it, good host? We cannot live forever but what we do, if loud enough, will echo throughout eternity. Good luck, good host, and thank you for taking the time to hear this old man's story.

THE WORLD IS M.A.G.I.C.K.A.L

MEMORIES are magickal moments in time
A treasure of the heart but kept in the mind

Remember those ANCESTORS that are now long gone
They are the magick that paved the road you are on

GENETICS are a scientific magickal mystery
Connected through time when making your own history

IMAGINATION is the inspiration we need
A breath of life, like a tree in the seed

CREATIVITY is the manifestation of things to be
The wonders of the mind brought to reality

KINSHIP is a treasure to help you through the times that are sad
An oath that we hold in life through the good moments and the bad

ASPIRATION is the fuel to ignite the fire
The pleasure, the pain, the will to achieve what we desire

One magickal thing that no one can explain
LOVE is the cause of so much joy and so much pain

HOld onto HOpe with HOnour everyday
To help you remember "Ho Ho Ho" along your way

Printed in Great Britain
by Amazon